Monday mornin̲. ... ̲ answer then.

Laurel's promise continued to haunt and shock him. All along, he'd thought she wouldn't hesitate to follow him to his new job. Now he wasn't so sure. What would he do if Laurel told him she didn't want to accept the job? Find another assistant to replace her?

He couldn't replace Laurel. He knew that and he figured she knew it, too. No one else would put up with his moods and demands the way she did. No one else would devote herself to his work as she did. And lastly, no one else at his side would feel right.

After what he'd been through, he never dreamed he'd allow his peace of mind to hinge on another woman. But here he was, agonizing over what Laurel might or might not do.

Had he lost his mind? Or was he just beginning to realize exactly what his assistant had come to mean to him?

Dear Reader,

Change, no matter what prompts it, is the thing that moves our lives from one direction to another. Sometimes we choose to make our own changes and other times they're forced upon us. Good or bad, how we deal with them reveals the sort of person we truly are.

Laurel has already experienced traumatic redirections in her life and she's decided her day-to-day rut of work, and little else, is the safest way to keep her heart from being crushed. As for Russ, he's already concluded that it's high time to move his life down a totally different trail. But will the woman he loves agree to follow him down that path to happiness? As you might guess, it's going to take some mighty big changes to get these two together.

Elsewhere, in Lincoln County, New Mexico, things are ever shifting. Babies are being born and new people are moving in! I hope you'll decide to join the Donovans and the Cantrells as they continue to help family and friends find love and happiness in the land of enchantment.

Thank you so much for reading, and God bless the trails you ride.

Stella

THE DOCTOR'S CALLING

STELLA BAGWELL

HARLEQUIN®
entertain, enrich, inspire™

Recycling programs
for this product may
not exist in your area.

ISBN-13: 978-0-373-65695-0

THE DOCTOR'S CALLING

STELLA BAGWELL

has written more than seventy novels for Harlequin and Silhouette Books. She credits her loyal readers and hopes her stories have brightened their lives in some small way.

A cowgirl through and through, she loves to watch old Westerns, and has recently learned how to rope a steer. Her days begin and end helping her husband care for a beloved herd of horses on their little ranch located on the south Texas coast. When she's not ropin' and ridin', you'll find her at her desk, creating her next tale of love.

The couple have a son, who is a high school math teacher and athletic coach. Stella loves to hear from readers and invites them to contact her at stellabagwell@gmail.com.

To our son, Jason,
and the changes he made for all of us
when he dropped a finger onto a map.
Love you!

Chapter One

"What did you say?"

As the question left Laurel Stanton's lips, she was transfixed on the man seated behind the large, messy desk. Dr. Russ Hollister had owned and operated Hollister Animal Clinic for twelve years, and Laurel had worked as his assistant for the past five of those. It was unimaginable to think her days with him were coming to an end.

His gaze locked on hers, he picked up a pen and tapped it absently against a stack of files. At thirty-eight years old, he was a tall, muscular man with big arms and hands to match. His shaggy blond hair was never combed and a dark five-o'clock shadow always covered the lower half of his face. But that was easily explainable, she thought. The man never had time to shave or get a decent haircut.

"Just what I said," he spoke with exaggerated patience. "As of January twenty-fifth, I'm taking the position of resident vet at the Chaparral Ranch. The Cantrell family owns the cattle and horse operation. I believe you're acquainted with them?"

Laurel had gone through high school and college with Alexa Cantrell. Now her friend lived in Texas with her Ranger husband and their children. Alexa's mother, Frankie, spent most of her time in Texas, too, where she had grown sons from a previous marriage. Only Quint, Alexa's brother, remained here in New Mexico to keep his late father's ranching dynasty going.

Laurel swallowed hard as a sinking weight hit the pit of her stomach. She'd noticed that Russ had been acting a bit unlike himself here lately, as though his mind were preoccupied with more than work, but she'd never dreamed he was about to do anything this drastic. What in the world could have come over him?

She said, "I've been friends with the Cantrells for years. They're great folks, but—"

Bewildered by it all, her voice trailed away, however, he seemed not to notice as he quickly replied, "That's one of the main reasons I decided to make this major job change. The family is trustworthy, solid and dependable. I can be sure that the ranch will always remain in their hands and I won't ever have to deal with the uncertainty of a new owner coming in and replacing me."

Being a resident vet for a prominent ranch like the Chaparral was an impressive position to hold. Plenty of veterinarians would give their eyeteeth for such a job, she thought. Besides the prestige, there would be many other advantages, such as not having to deal with tons of paperwork, the demands of the public and traveling all over the county in the middle of the night. Still, Russ had always been his own boss. It was hard for her to imagine an independent guy like him willing to be an employee rather than the other way around.

"But you own this clinic," she reasoned. "Your business is so great that you can't handle it all. Why—"

Before she could get the whole question out, he interrupted, "That's right. I can't handle it all. It's grown to be too much for you and me to deal with."

Questions and doubts tumbled through her mind as her gaze slipped over his rugged features. She'd never thought of Russ Hollister as a handsome man. He was too rough around the edges for that description. But he was sexy as all get-out and totally unaware of the fact, which made him even more unbearably attractive.

Five years ago, when he'd first hired her, he'd been a married man. But three years later, that had all changed when divorce had parted him from a classy, career-driven wife. Ever since then, Laurel tried not to think of him in terms of being "available." He was nothing more to her than her boss, or, from the sound of things, soon to be former boss.

Pressing fingertips against her puckered forehead, she tried to put her concerns into words. "I realize you're overworked and—"

"We're both overworked," he corrected.

"Okay. I agree. You have to deal with people and things that would frazzle the nerves of a saint, but this place and all the animals—who will care for them? You've been here—"

"I don't need for you to tell me how long I've been here, Laurel. The floors in this old building are stained with my blood and sweat. But that's soon ending. I'll be leaving the end of next week. And Dr. Brennan will be taking over shortly afterward. So there's no need for you to worry. The horses from the track and all the other animals around here won't go without a vet."

But what about her? What about the long, arduous hours she'd invested in this clinic? In him? Were they all for naught? She wanted to fling the questions at him.

This isn't about him or what he means to you, Laurel. This is about your job, your livelihood, the sum of what makes up your life. This isn't about your personal feelings.

Russ was a demanding boss who spoke bluntly and, more often than not, took her for granted. But he was also honest and fair. And where animals were concerned, his heart was as big as Texas. It wasn't enough for him to simply cure a patient from illness or injury. He always went a step further to make sure the animal would remain healthy and happy. There was never a time he put himself before the welfare of his patients. She admired him greatly, and though he often irked her with his caustic tongue, once she'd begun working for him, she'd never considered working for anyone else. She was hopelessly devoted and attached to the man.

Suddenly feeling weak in the knees, Laurel sank into one of the hard metal chairs that were normally reserved for pet owners. But it was eight o'clock at night—far past closing hours—and the building was empty, except for him, her and the few cats and dogs that remained at the clinic for more extensive care.

"I see," she said, her voice low and hoarse, then asked, "Does Dr. Brennan have an assistant?"

Shrugging, he leaned back in the wide leather chair, and the indifference she saw on his face made her wish she had the guts to reach over and pop her palm against his jaw.

"I haven't questioned the man about his staff," he said frankly. "That's his business."

After five years, Laurel was used to his curtness, and most of the time she ignored it. But his announcement had knocked her for a loop. She wasn't in any mood for sarcasm.

Her back teeth grinding together, she quickly rose to her feet. "Well, did you ever think it might have been more thoughtful to let me in on this a bit sooner? Jobs aren't exactly hanging from tree limbs right now. But I suppose I'm just an afterthought in all of this."

He arched a brow at her. "Sit down."

The quietly spoken command made her hackles rise. "Why? I still have work to do before we close up. And I'd like to get to bed before midnight."

"I'm not finished with this conversation yet. That's why." He pointed to the vacated chair as though she was a child instead of a thirty-year-old woman, and it was on the tip of her tongue to tell him what an ass he could sometimes be. After all, her job was coming to an end. But what else could he do to her, she asked herself. Fire her before the week was out? The thought sent a bubble of hysterical laughter rising in her throat, and she realized she was very close to breaking down in front of this man who had little to no patience for weakness in human beings. Yet he had a massive heart where animals were concerned.

Biting back a weary sigh, she sank into the still-warm seat. "Okay. Lay it on me," she invited with a fatal dose of sarcasm.

He frowned. "First of all, I didn't share all of this with you earlier, because I knew you'd be upset."

She sputtered in disbelief. "Upset! That's putting it mildly. I'm going along thinking my job is secure and you spring this on me! Wouldn't any normal person be upset?"

He didn't say anything for a moment, and she suddenly felt his gaze roaming her face and hair. She had no doubt her gray eyes were sparking fire and her cheeks were pink. As for the rest of her, she was certain she looked as tired as she felt. Her long chestnut hair had loosened from its thick, single braid and now hung raggedly against the front of her left shoulder. What little makeup she'd applied this morning had been washed away by the early-morning drizzle that had fallen while she and Russ had trudged into a cattle pen to treat a bull with an infected horn. Her blue jeans and green-plaid flannel shirt could no longer be deemed clean, and her black cowboy boots were caked with dried red mud.

It was rare that Russ ever took the time to really look at her, and Laurel never fussed with her appearance. Not for him or any man. But now as she faced him in the dimly lit office, she realized his warm brown eyes made her feel quite uncomfortable and very much like a woman.

Since he was making no effort to speak, she decided to do it for him, saying, "Don't bother to answer. I shouldn't have said any of that. This is your clinic. What you do or don't do with it is entirely your business. I'm just an employee."

So why did she feel like so much more? she wondered, her spirits as dead as the potted plant in the window behind his head. Maybe it was the fifty or sixty hours she spent every week with this man. Maybe it was the emotional ups and downs she'd gone through as the two of them had lost and saved animals of all types, ages and sizes.

A grimace creased his broad forehead and pressed

his hard lips into a crooked line. "Do you think you can manage to be quiet for two minutes?"

"I don't know," she quipped. "Do we have the time to do a test?"

He tossed down the pen and used the hand to rake a path through his sandy-blond hair. "If you'd shut up, I might be able to explain that I've not forgotten you in all of this. Do you think I'd just heartlessly dismiss you without any warning?"

She didn't think he was heartless. He showed love and kindness to the animals every day. Just not to her. But then, he wasn't that sort of man. And she was his assistant, not his girlfriend, she reminded herself.

Swallowing a sigh, she blurted, "I've never been able to read your mind. So I can hardly know what's in it now."

His nostrils flaring, he darted her a sharp look. "Good thing," he muttered, then shook his head with something like self-disgust. "I don't know why in hell I've put up with you all these years. Or why in hell I want you to go with me. You're a pain. A big, fat pain. But the truth is I don't want to work without you."

That last shocking remark straightened her spine and scooted her butt to the edge of the chair. "Work! Without me? What are you talking about?"

"The Chaparral," he snapped with impatience. "I want you to remain my assistant. I will need one there. Or hadn't that crossed your mind?"

All sorts of things had been rolling through her mind these past few minutes, she thought. But nothing like this!

She glanced at the watch on her wrist. "It's been less than five minutes since you've sprung this news on me. I haven't had time to think about anything!"

He deliberately swung his attention to the clock on his desk. Once the second hand made a complete sweep of the numbers, he said, "Okay. You've had five minutes now. What do you think?"

Her insides were suddenly trembling, and she quickly clasped her hands together to keep them from outwardly shaking.

"First of all, the Cantrells offered you a job. Not me. And secondly, the ranch is several miles west of Ruidoso, and part of the trip is over rough, graveled road. The commute there would take at least forty-five minutes one way. That's—"

"The Cantrells have already agreed to hire you—if you want the job," he quickly interrupted. "And you wouldn't be commuting. You'd be living there—on the ranch. Just like I will be."

He was leaving his large home in the suburbs and moving to the ranch? And the Cantrells were offering her a job and a place to stay, too? Something was wrong with this picture. She'd not spoken to Alexa in several weeks, but that didn't mean her old friend might not be pulling strings. As grateful as Laurel was for the offer, she'd been independent since—well, since she was a little girl. She didn't want handouts from anyone. And she especially didn't want to be hired because Russ had made stipulations to include her.

"I find all of this hard to believe. I mean, I believe the part about you—I'm sure the Cantrells were willing to offer you the moon to get you to work for them. But me—the ranch hardly needs my services."

Leaning forward, he pulled a card from a Rolodex and tossed it on the desk in front of her. "If you don't believe me, call Quint and talk with him. I'm sure he can answer any questions you might have."

Quint Cantrell was Alexa's younger brother. And since their father, Lewis, had died several years ago, he was now the man in charge of the ranch. Through her friendship with Alexa, she knew him quite well. But she didn't want to talk with him tonight. She needed time to calm herself, to think about what all of this was going to do to her life.

"I'm not sure I have any questions for Quint," she said after a moment. "Because I'm not at all sure I want to take the job."

Surprise flickered in his eyes, but he couldn't be any more surprised than she was at herself. The words had popped out of her mouth with a will of their own, as though something inside her had plucked the remark straight out of the chaos going on in her head.

Long seconds stretched in the quiet room before he finally asked, "You aren't interested in the job?"

"I didn't say that. I said I wasn't sure about it," she corrected.

"You were just bemoaning the fact that jobs weren't hanging from tree limbs. You have something else in mind that you'd rather do?"

She resisted the urge to squirm upon the seat. There had been times in the past when she'd thought of moving on to work for another vet or changing to a different job that still involved caring for animals. Anything to get her away from the hopeless attachment she felt toward Russ. But she'd never been strong enough to take such a step.

"Not exactly," she answered vaguely. "But moving to the Chaparral—that would be a major move for me."

"I'm well aware of that," he said bluntly. "It's a major move for me, too."

"That's true," she reluctantly agreed. "But it's different for you."

"How so?"

Groaning wearily, she scrubbed her face with both hands. "I don't want to talk about this anymore tonight, Russ. I'll think about it and give you my decision tomorrow."

"Tomorrow is Sunday. You don't work on Sundays, remember?"

Only because she'd demanded that he give her that one day off. Otherwise, she'd be working nonstop for seven days a week. As for Russ, he had to come to the clinic no matter what day of the week it was. There were always small animals to be cared for and fed, and then there were the horses and cattle penned in the shelters behind the building that needed the same attention. Sometimes she took pity on him and showed up on Sunday afternoons to help him. And though he'd never said he appreciated her gesture, he always added overtime pay to her weekly check.

But money or salary from Russ had never been an issue with Laurel. All she'd ever really wanted from him was his appreciation, along with a little thoughtfulness. And his companionship throughout the workday. Unfortunately, the latter had become the thing she wanted from him most of all.

"All right then, I'll phone you."

"No. You won't phone me," he said flatly. "You're going to give me your decision directly to my face."

It was just like him to make something as difficult as possible for her, she thought crossly. "Okay. Monday morning. I'll give you my answer then."

She started out of the small room, but before she could slip out the door, he called out her name.

Pausing, Laurel looked back at him and for one brief moment she wanted to burst into tears. She wanted to beat her fist against his chest and ask him why he was doing this to her. She'd never been good with changes. She'd been through too many tough ones to ever dream a good change could come into her life.

"Don't bother about cleaning up the operating room. I'll deal with that and anything else that we left undone. Go on home."

He'd never given her a break like this before and she wondered why he was making such a gesture tonight. Because their time in this clinic was nearly over? Because their days of working together were almost at an end?

They didn't have to end, she thought. She had a choice. She could follow the man to the Chaparral. But would that be the right and healthy thing for her to do?

Suddenly her throat was burning, and when she spoke her voice was unusually hoarse. "Thanks, Russ," she said simply. "I'll see you Monday morning."

It was nearing midnight when Russ maneuvered his four-wheel-drive truck over the snow-packed driveway leading up to the house he'd called home for the past twelve years. The large split-level brick structure was situated on the eastern edge of Ruidoso Downs and had a beautiful view of Sierra Blanca. Though it was far from being a mansion, it was a comfortable, spacious house with more amenities than Russ wanted or needed.

He was basically a simple man and had only purchased the property because his ex-wife, Brooke, had insisted it was a fitting home for a doctor.

Doctor, hell, he mentally snorted. He wasn't a doctor. He was a vet. But she'd never wanted or tried to see the difference. She'd had huge ambitions for him and herself. And in the end, he supposed those ambitions were the very things that had split them apart. As for the house they'd once shared, he'd remained in it simply because it was much easier than moving, and it was close to his clinic. Besides, the rooms didn't hold many memories, good or bad, of their marriage. The time they'd spent together within its walls had been very limited.

But Russ rarely thought of Brooke anymore, or their ill-fated relationship. At least, he'd not thought of her until about a month ago when he'd spotted her in a restaurant in downtown Ruidoso. Once they'd divorced and she'd moved away, Russ hadn't seen her in the area. But she had longtime friends here, so it wasn't really a surprise to see her dining with old acquaintances. Especially since it had been during the Christmas holiday season. No, the surprise had been Brooke's obvious pregnancy.

She'd never been willing to give him a child. But apparently the new man in her life had changed her mind about becoming a mother. And that idea had jolted him, had left him wondering just what his life and work were all about.

After parking his truck in the garage, he entered the house through a side door leading into the kitchen. Inside the warm room, he shrugged out of his heavy jacket and slung it over a chair. At the refrigerator, he pulled out a longneck beer and twisted off the cap.

He rarely consumed alcohol, especially not cold beer on a winter night. But right now he was feeling the need to blunt the image of Laurel's face. Earlier this evening, when he'd told her he was closing the clinic, he felt he'd never seen such utter disappointment on anyone's face. And that alone bothered the hell out of Russ.

He'd always been an independent person. He lived to suit himself and made his own decisions on what he thought best, not what someone else believed. For the past two years Quint Cantrell had been encouraging Russ to become the Chaparral's resident vet. In fact, the ranch owner had vowed he wouldn't fill the position until Russ was ready and certain he wanted to accept the job.

During that time, Russ had weighed the offer, asking himself if selling his clinic and moving to the Chaparral was the right thing for him to do. Working exclusively for the ranch would simplify his life and allow him to do the work he loved under much easier conditions. It would give him time in his life to do more than simply caring for animals from sunup to sundown, and falling exhausted into bed every night, only to get up and start all over again. He wanted time for a home and family. All those reasons had been weighing heavily on him, but he'd been reluctant to make changes. Until he'd seen his ex-wife pregnant. She'd clearly moved on, and it was time that he did, too.

He truly believed that selling the clinic and moving to the Chaparral was a step in the right direction for himself and for Laurel. In spite of what his devoted assistant thought, he had considered her in this move. After all, he wasn't blind. He'd been watching her work herself to a weary stupor day after day, and this change in jobs would ease the load on her shoulders, too. But there simply hadn't been any option of taking on more staff or a partner. Now he wanted that easier life for Laurel just as much as he wanted it for himself. Yet it was plain she wasn't happy about any of this, and now he was beginning to wonder if he had the woman figured all wrong, or even worse, if he'd taken her for granted.

A loud meow at his feet drew Russ's attention downward. A coal-black Tiffany with long hair and big green eyes was giving him a look of disgust.

"What do you want, Leo? You've got food in your bowl. Look right here." Russ walked over to the automatic feeder and pointed to the mound of dry morsels. "And I'm not about to open a can of salmon for you tonight."

The cat marched over to a nearby cabinet, sat back on his haunches and pawed at the handle. Russ cursed beneath his breath. The damn cat was spoiled and too smart for his own good. "Listen, you little black monster, you wouldn't even be in this house if it wasn't for Laurel. You'd be out on the streets begging—no, I take that back—you wouldn't even be alive if she hadn't picked you up from that cold alley. You would've died from distemper. Maybe you ought to be thinking how fortunate you are instead of demanding fish or liver every night."

The cat shot him a bored look, then pawed at the door again. "You ungrateful feline," Russ muttered at him. "Maybe when I move to the ranch I'll just leave you behind. What do think about that?"

Even as he made the threat to Leo, he knew that no matter where he lived, the cat would always have a home with him. A year ago Laurel had arrived at work early one morning, carrying in a limp ball of black fur, its eyes and nose covered with dried infection and so weak he could barely make a faint meowing noise. His lungs were in distress, plus he was dehydrated and starved. Russ didn't think the animal had much chance of surviving, but Laurel had begged him to try. They'd hooked him up on an IV, shot him full of antibiotics and made sure he was warm. After that there hadn't been much left to do except wait and pray.

After two days, and a great deal of Laurel's nursing, the cat began to improve. Eventually he recovered enough to be adopted out, and Russ had expected Laurel to be the first one to offer the feline a home. After all, she seemed crazy about the animal and she already had two dogs and three other cats. One more mouth to feed wouldn't make that much difference. But she'd stunned him by suggesting that Russ take Leo home with him.

At first he'd laughed and scoffed at the idea. Russ didn't have pets. He dealt with enough animals throughout the day to go home and contend with another at night. But she'd continued to hound him by arguing that Russ needed the cat and the cat needed Russ.

He didn't know why he'd given in to her and brought the cat home. Most of the time he and Leo merely tolerated each other, but he had to admit there were times, like tonight, when Russ was glad the house wasn't empty and there was someone here who actually needed him.

"All right, so I'm bluffing and you know it," he muttered to Leo. "But you're still not getting salmon. Just a few treats, that's all. You're getting too fat."

He doled out a few moist morsels to the cat, then fetched his beer from the table and carried it into the den. A television sat in one corner of the long, comfortably furnished room, but he didn't bother switching it on. The only thing he ever watched was the news and weather, and even that didn't interest him tonight.

Monday morning. I'll give you my answer then.

Laurel's promise continued to haunt and shock him. All along, he'd thought she wouldn't hesitate to follow him to his new job. Now he wasn't so sure. What would he do if Laurel told him she didn't want to accept the job at the Chaparral? Find another assistant to replace her?

Hell. He couldn't replace Laurel. He knew that and he figured she knew it, too. No one else would put up with his moods and demands the way she did. No one else would devote herself to his work the way she did. And lastly, no one else at his side would feel right.

He was staring thoughtfully into the quiet shadows when Leo suddenly jumped into his lap and stared expectantly up at him.

"I don't know, boy. Maybe I've made a mistake." He placed the beer aside and stroked a hand down Leo's arched back. "But you proved me wrong when you survived. If I'm lucky, Laurel will prove me wrong and take the job. If she refuses my offer—well, I don't know what I'll do."

Leo meowed as though he understood, and Russ groaned.

After the hell Brooke had put him through, he'd never dreamed he'd allow his peace of mind to hinge on another woman. But here he was, agonizing over what Laurel might or might not do.

Had he lost his mind? Or was he just beginning to realize exactly what his assistant had come to mean to him?

He was afraid to answer that.

Chapter Two

The next day, in a small apartment across town, Laurel stuffed another load of clothes into the washing machine, then picked up a portable phone from the breakfast bar in the kitchen. Since it was late in the afternoon, she hoped she'd timed the call so that Alexa Redman was finished with church services and Sunday dinner with her loved ones.

Her friend answered on the third ring and Laurel quickly apologized for interrupting her weekend.

"Don't be silly, Laurel. I was wondering if you were ever going to return my last call."

Laurel sighed. "Sorry I haven't gotten back to you before now, Alexa. Work, you know. It never lets up."

"Friends don't have to apologize to each other for being busy," Alexa assured her in a cheery voice. "How's the weather there? Freezing?"

Alexa and her family lived on a ranch located near

San Antonio, and from what her friend had told her, the winters there were extremely mild compared to Ruidoso and Lincoln County.

"There's snow on the ground, but the sun is out. I paid the little neighbor boy five dollars to clear my driveway, but he left a huge drift right in the middle."

Alexa laughed. "What do you expect for five dollars?" she teased, then went on with another, more pertinent question. "So how have you been?"

Laurel bit back a sigh. "Busy. Exhausted. Confused."

Alexa latched onto to Laurel's last word. "Confused about what? I hope this means you've finally gotten a man in your life."

Laurel's last date had been more than three years ago, and she'd only gone then as a favor to a friend, not because she'd been interested in the guy. She didn't date or socialize, especially in a serious manner. She'd decided a long time ago that having a family was not for her.

Rolling her eyes, Laurel eased a hip onto one of the barstools and asked, "When would I have time for a man? And why would I want one?"

Alexa muttered an unladylike curse beneath her breath. "To have a family, that's why!"

As always, when someone mentioned the word *family,* something went cold and stiff inside Laurel. Her mother had left the Stanton family years ago, while her father and brother had never really included her in their lives, especially after both of them had moved to Arizona. Laurel's twin sister, Lainey, had died when the girls were only fourteen. But that was something she didn't like to discuss with anyone, even Alexa.

"I have a family in Tucson, such as they are," she said flatly. "My father and brother."

"That's not the sort of family I'm talking about, and you know it."

"Look, Alexa, I didn't call to hash out the subject of marriage with you. I've called to ask you about my job."

"Your job? Don't tell me that you've finally gotten enough of Doc Hollister's taskmaster attitude?"

Laurel grimaced at the hopeful surprise in Alexa's voice. Even though she often called Russ a devil to work for, she didn't like hearing someone else label him. Above everything, he was a very dedicated and wonderful doctor.

"You must not know anything about Russ going to work for the Chaparral," Laurel replied.

"What?"

"Dr. Hollister is taking a position on the Chaparral. You haven't talked with Quint about this?"

"We've discussed the issue of getting a resident vet for the ranch for some time now. And I was in total agreement with my brother when he said Russ was a candidate. But I left the details of hiring up to him. He's the expert and I trust him implicitly to pick the right person for the job."

"Oh. Well, that right person appears to be Russ."

"Hmm. That's great news."

"Great news?" Laurel quickly blurted the question. "You just called the man a taskmaster."

"Yes. But I couldn't count the times you've told me how wonderful he is with animals. That's the kind of vet the Chaparral needs, and clearly my brother thinks so, too." After a thoughtful pause, she went on, "Oh, I see where you're going with this now. The clinic. He'll no longer be running it."

Laurel felt sick with uncertainty. "He's selling the

place. A new vet is taking over soon—a Dr. Brennan from Alamogordo."

"So you'll be working for this new person?"

Closing her eyes, Laurel stuttered, "I—uh—no. I don't think so. Russ seems to think the man is bringing his own staff with him."

"Oh, Laurel," Alexa groaned. "I'm so sorry about this. I know how much you've poured your heart and soul into that place. Dear God, you must be devastated over this development. But surely you can get hired on at another veterinary office somewhere in or near Ruidoso."

Laurel swallowed. "Actually, I already have a job offer. Russ wants me to accompany him to the Chaparral. He says that Quint is willing to hire me, too. When Russ first told me this I thought you'd done some finagling to get me a job. But now it's clear that you're not involved."

Her friend was quiet for so long that Laurel finally asked, "Are you still there, Alexa?"

"Sorry. I was just thinking what a smart brother I have."

"But Alexa, I'm not sure about any of this! Russ says the ranch will supply my housing. Can you imagine me living all the way out there? In the wilds?"

Alexa chuckled. "Why not? It's where I lived for years, and I turned out to be a reasonably sane person. Although Jonas might disagree about that sometimes," she added jokingly of her husband.

As if on cue, Laurel could hear a child's loud squeal in the background and then the *tap, tap* of running footsteps followed by more shouts and squeals.

"Hang on, Laurel. I've got to put down the phone."

While Alexa was away from the phone, Laurel imagined her disciplining her small son and daughter with a firm but loving hand. Just the way a child should be handled, she thought, as loss and regret stabbed her deep.

Years ago, she and her twin had both dreamed and planned, like most young girls their age, of growing up and having babies of their own. But that had been before Lainey came down with a blood disease. That had been before she and her twin had been deserted by their mother and neglected by a weak-willed father. Now Lainey was dead and Laurel's dreams of having a family of her own had died along with her.

"Sorry, Laurel," Alexa said when she finally returned to the phone. "The kids were playing tag in the house. I shooed them outside."

"Don't apologize. I need to let you go."

"Not before you tell me what you plan to do about your job."

Laurel sighed. "I'm not sure—oh, God, Alexa, maybe I should use this opportunity to move on and work for someone else."

After a long pause, Alexa said thoughtfully, "I couldn't count the times you've told me that you'd like to wring Dr. Hollister's neck. On the other hand, you clearly admire him. If not, you wouldn't have worked for him this long."

"Five years and counting," Laurel said dully. "And now—it's either follow him or end everything."

Silent moments passed before Alexa finally said, "Sounds to me like you're talking about a personal relationship instead of a working one."

A hot flush swept over Laurel's face and she thanked

God that her friend couldn't see her. "Look, Alexa, outside of work, Russ doesn't know I exist."

"You're young and attractive," Alexa argued. "You could change that if you wanted to."

"That's just the point. I don't want to change anything. I want things to stay just as they are."

"You have all the ingredients to be a good wife and mother. Instead you want to cling to the past, to believe you're unworthy of anyone's love."

"I don't expect you to understand what I've gone through with my family. And it's too complicated to explain. But when Lainey became ill, I lost everything—even my childhood. I can't deal with more losing. If I move on to another job, I'll forget Russ. And in the end that would be better for both of us."

"Would it?"

Laurel closed her eyes. "At least I'll never be hurt."

"You'll never really live, either."

"If I didn't love you, I'd slam this phone down and never speak to you again," Laurel said in a low, strained voice. "But I do love you. Even though you don't understand me."

"Okay, Laurel, let's make this simple. Do you like working with Russ and believe your job is worthwhile?"

Laurel groaned as the conflicting emotions inside her continued to battle back and forth. "I need to decide if I'm going to move on or simply hang on?"

"Why bother?" Alexa asked with annoyance. "You're not going to let yourself get involved, so working with Dr. Hollister is the safest place you can be."

Safe? Laurel never felt safe when she was around Russ. He was a constant pull on her heartstrings, a constant reminder of how lonely she'd become. "That's so crazy it almost makes sense."

Alexa chuckled. "Grandfather Abe gave me my brains. But don't tell him I said so."

Later, after the two women had said goodbye, Laurel walked to her bedroom where a photo of her and Lainey sat on a dressing table. The two girls were standing in front of the family Christmas tree, dressed identically in jeans and red sweaters, with reindeer antlers on their heads. They were hugging each other close, their smiles full of childish, ten-year-olds' giggles.

At that time, the two girls had been happy, normal sisters, swapping clothes and whispering about boys. Four years later, Lainey's death had shattered Laurel's world, and for years afterward, she'd believed she would never feel much about anything or anyone. She'd finished high school, gone through college and even tried to date and pretend to have all the basic needs and wants of a normal young woman. But she'd only been going through the motions. Then she'd gone to work for Russ, and slowly everything began to change. She'd began to feel again, to want and dream again. But along with those wonderful feelings had come doubts and fears.

Oh, Lainey. If you were here now, maybe I would be a stronger woman. Maybe I'd have the courage and confidence to reach out for the things my heart really longs for.

Her heart heavy, she set the frame back on the dresser as Alexa's words whispered through her thoughts.

Working with Dr. Hollister is the safest place you can be.

Maybe that was why being with him was the only place she wanted to be, Laurel thought dismally. Because there wasn't any danger of him asking her to be a wife or mother.

* * *

Early Monday morning when Russ parked his truck behind the clinic, gray winter clouds were shrouding the nearby mountains and a north wind rattled the bare limbs on the lone aspen standing next to the brick building. Several yards away, near one of the holding pens, Laurel's truck was already parked and, though she always arrived early, she was never this early.

Grabbing up a bag of medical tools from the passenger seat, he departed the truck and quickly entered the building. Inside, the scent of freshly brewed coffee wafted down the hallway from the tiny room they used as a kitchen. Russ strode straight toward the smell, while glancing first one way and then the other at the open doorways of the examining rooms.

He eventually found Laurel in the recovery room, checking on a German shepherd he'd operated on Friday evening for a broken leg. The moment she heard his footsteps, she glanced around and smiled.

No matter what was going on, she always started the day by giving him a smile, and although he'd never told her so, the sight always lifted his spirits. She was a distant sort of woman who didn't invite much personal exchange with him or anyone. When he'd first hired her, he'd believed her attitude was reserved only for him, but over the years, he'd come to see that she was an extremely private person. Oddly, though, when it came to work, she was more than quick to spar words with him.

Along with her smile, Russ liked the fact that she wasn't afraid to stand up to him, no matter what he threw at her. But he'd never told her that, either. Russ figured after five years she should know he appreciated her work. Otherwise he would have replaced her long ago. Now he feared he'd been lax about letting her know that he needed her.

"Good morning," she greeted him.

"Morning," he replied as he moved across the room to where she stood by the shepherd's cage.

"How is she?" he asked while inclining his head toward the dog.

"I'm impressed. She's already eaten everything I've given her and drunk her water. And when I first walked in, I found her standing."

He nodded with approval. "I could see a spark of survival in her eyes yesterday. She's going to do just fine."

Laurel gave the dog one last pat on the head, then carefully secured the door on the cage. As she turned to move away, Russ caught the fresh, sweet fragrance she always wore. The woman rarely bothered to put lipstick or any other color on her face, but she always smelled very feminine.

Now, why in heck had that sort of thing entered his mind this morning? he wondered. He thought of Laurel as his helper and friend who just happened to be female, and nothing more. That's how, after all these years, he'd made sure their working relationship stayed strong.

"If you're hungry, there are breakfast tacos in the kitchen. And I just brewed a pot of coffee."

Russ started to tell her he'd already eaten, but she walked out of the room before he had a chance to speak, leaving him little choice but to follow her. Damn it, what was she doing, trying to make him sweat for her decision?

Down the narrow hallway, he saw her duck into the tiny kitchen and by the time he entered the room, she was already pouring herself a mug of coffee.

"Have you forgotten something?" he asked as he

rested a hip on a tiny wooden table pushed against one wall.

She glanced over her shoulder at him, and the innocent arch of her brows made him want to let out a frustrated groan.

"Was I supposed to bring something to work with me this morning?"

Russ was doing his best to remain cool, even though he was nervous and worried. Which was a hell of an admission for him. Nothing ever unnerved him and he'd long ago learned that worrying was a waste of time and effort. Yet this uncertainty with Laurel had him behaving completely out of character. "Come on, Laurel, you know that I'm waiting for your answer about the job."

She plopped two cubes of sugar into her coffee mug and stirred. "All right. But before I give it to you, I want to know about Maccoy. Friday night when we were discussing this, I forgot to ask about him. What's going to happen to his job?"

Maccoy acted as the receptionist/bookkeeper and also kept all medications stocked and accounted for. In his seventies now, he'd once been a saddle bronc rider on the rodeo circuit, but a horrific spill toward the end of his career had broken his back and left him limping on his left leg. But the handicap was nothing to Maccoy. He could still work circles around three men.

"You needn't worry about Maccoy. He draws a disability check."

Outraged, she let out a loud gasp. "You know that Maccoy is a man that wants to be productive. He wants to work!"

He gave her a wry little grin. "I'm only kidding. I called him yesterday. Maccoy is going to the ranch, along with me. He's very happy about it, too, I might add. He'll be living in the bunkhouse with a few of the single ranch hands, so he'll have company at night and he can cut out the high rent he pays now."

She looked at him through long, dark lashes. It wasn't often that he teased or joked. Apparently, just the thought of this new job had lifted his spirits. "So he'll still be working with us?"

Russ nodded. "That's right. Doing the same thing he's doing now, except he won't have to answer the phone a jillion times a day to deal with appointments and hysterical pet owners."

She outwardly sighed. "That's good. I'm glad."

"You were actually worried about him?"

Frowning now, she said, "Why wouldn't I be concerned? I've worked with him all these years. I'm fond of the old man."

"You've worked with me for years, too. But you hardly seem concerned for me." Now, why the hell had he made that remark? He didn't want Laurel's care or attention. He just wanted her excellent work as an assistant.

She actually laughed. "Russ, I think you're a man who's perfectly capable of taking care of himself."

He always had, he thought grimly. From the time he'd been a young teenager, he'd pretty much had to scrape for himself. Once his mother and father had divorced, his father, Curt, had left for parts unknown. Nanette, his mother, God bless her soul, had done the best she could to care for herself and her young son. But about the time of Russ's seventeenth birthday, she'd developed cancer and without the funds for proper treatment and the support of family, she'd succumbed quickly to the disease. After that, Russ had gone to live with Nanette's brother, who'd lived in Albuquerque at the time.

But Russ's uncle had been a bachelor, who'd been far more comfortable nursing a cheap bottle of wine than dealing with a teenage boy.

As a result, Russ had learned a guy had to take care of himself. No one else was going to do it for him, much less do it the right way. Before his mother had died, Russ had promised her he would continue his quest to be a veterinarian, and once she was gone, he was even more determined to achieve the goal.

With the help of scholarships for good grades, he'd worked his way through college. Then after he'd finally earned his license to practice veterinary medicine, he'd slowly paid off all his debts and eventually purchased this clinic near the racetrack in Ruidoso. Hollister Animal Clinic had given him a more than nice living; he had earned a great living. But the workload was staggering and the money not worth the toll it was taking on him physically and mentally.

"You're right, I can take care of myself. But I do need an assistant. What's your decision?"

Breaking eye contact with him, she turned back to the coffeepot. "I'll be going with you. After all these years, I know what you want and expect. Another vet would probably do everything differently and I'd have to learn all over again. And I don't like changes," she reasoned.

He stared at her back and wondered if anything else had persuaded her to follow him to the Chaparral. Such as the fact that she might actually *enjoy* working with him. But that was hardly an important factor, and he didn't know why the idea had even entered his mind. It should be enough that she was going to continue to work for him.

"Good," he said. "I hope you'll be happy with your decision."

That brought her head around, and she stared at him with skeptical amusement. "Since when has the word *happy* ever entered your mind? Much less your vocabulary?" she asked.

"Happy?" he repeated blankly. "That's nothing new for me. I'm a basically happy man. And I want everybody else to be happy, too."

Disbelief twisted her plush lips, and for a brief moment he wondered if she'd ever kissed a man. Kissed him with real passion. He'd never heard her talk about dating or having a boyfriend. But that didn't mean she stayed home and alone every night of her life. The only things they discussed were work and weather and sometimes politics. But since that last topic usually caused an eruption of fireworks, he tried to avoid it.

"You've got to be kidding," she muttered. "You, happy? I've never seen it."

He didn't know how the back-and-forth of their conversation had taken on a personal tone. Or why his thoughts kept turning to intimate questions about his assistant. Whatever the reason, it was high time to put an end to it.

Rising to his full height, he brushed past her and quickly went about filling a heavy mug with coffee. "I'll be driving out to the Chaparral tomorrow evening. You might want to go along and see the house where you'll be living," he suggested. "I'm sure you'll want to see what furniture you'll need to make the place comfortable."

"A house! I'll have a house all to myself?"

Her surprise prompted him to glance at her, and the

look of joyous wonder he saw on her face made him feel
as though he'd finally done something right in her eyes.

"What else?"

The smile on her face went from ear to ear and displayed her perfect white teeth. It was rare to ever see
such a glowing look on her face, and Russ could hardly
keep from staring.

She said, "I figured I'd get a room at the back of the
ranch house, or a cubbyhole in one of the nearby buildings that would only be big enough for eating and sleeping. Certainly not a house. This is incredible!"

Before he realized her intentions, she flung her
arms around him and hugged him tightly. The contact
of her body next to his momentarily shocked him, and
all Russ could do was think about the way her breasts
were smashed against his chest, and the way her soft
cheek was pressed against his.

"Oh, thank you, Russ! This makes everything so
much more bearable."

"You're welcome," he murmured, but Russ doubted
that she'd heard his reply. She'd already pulled away
from him and was rushing out the door. He quickly
called after her. "Where are you going?"

"To tell Maccoy about this!"

The excitement in her voice filtered back to him,
and for a moment Russ stood in the middle of the tiny
kitchen and smiled to himself. He hadn't realized what
having a house of her own would mean to her. Nor had
he realized what having her in his arms would mean
to him.

*It was just a thank-you hug, Russ. A brief expression
of gratitude. Forget it.*

With a little effort, he might be able to forget the
sweet pleasure of having her cheek pressed to his. But

even if he lived to be an old man, he'd never forget the relief that had poured through him when she'd told him she would be going with him to the Chaparral.

What in heck was this change in job, this move, doing to him?

He wanted to believe his relief stemmed from the fact that she was the best assistant he'd ever worked with, and he didn't want to lose such a top-notch employee.

But as Russ swiftly strode toward his office, he realized all this relief he was feeling came from the fact that he was still going to have Laurel in his life. Period.

Chapter Three

Even though Maccoy was doing his best to taper off the appointments for the last remaining days of the clinic, it was still late the next evening before Laurel and Russ finished with the last patient and locked up the clinic.

By the time the two of them climbed into Russ's truck to make the trip to the Chaparral, the winter sun was long gone and darkness had urged the streetlights to flicker on. The weather had made a turn for the worst, with a sheet of snowflakes flying in front of the headlights' beams.

Russ said, "This doesn't look like the best weather to make the trip, but waiting for it to get better might take days." He glanced across the console separating their seats to see that Laurel was bundled in a heavy green sweater with a bright plaid scarf wrapped around her neck. A thick parka lay on her lap, and he realized that during all the time that she'd worked for him, whether they'd had to deal with rain or snow, cold or heat, she always seemed to be prepared and never complained.

"Your truck is four-wheel drive. We've made a lot rougher trips in much worse weather," she remarked. "Remember when old man Nobles called us out to his place to help his mare foal? There must have been two feet of snow on the ground then."

He nodded. "Yeah. I think we hit the ditch about three or four times before we ever got there."

A fond smile touched her face. "Yes, but we got there in time and the mare delivered a beautiful little filly. It had a tiny white snip on its nose and one white sock."

"We've delivered hundreds of foals around here. How do you remember that one so well?"

"Because that night I was so afraid we weren't going to get there in time for you to turn the foal. I guess the fear made everything about that night stick in my mind."

Surprised by her admission, he glanced at her. In all of their emergency encounters, she'd never panicked or shown a hint of fear. To hear her admit to being afraid back then made him wonder what other sort of emotions she might be masking now. "You never let on that you were afraid," he said.

"I wouldn't let myself. I wanted to be the best help I could be. Not a weepy, hand-wringing female."

No, he thought, even when death was looming, Laurel was strong and dependable, like a steadying handhold on a slippery slope. Funny, but she was the exact opposite of his ex-wife, who'd fallen to pieces over a simple cut on her finger.

But then, Brooke was an entirely different person from Laurel. She was different from him, too. And now, looking back on his courtship and marriage, he wondered what had drawn him to the woman in the first place. Oh, she'd been pretty, all right. Her bobbed brown hair had always been fixed and smooth, her clothes tailored and perfect, her makeup subtle and classic. She wasn't from a rich, socially active family, but compared to his, her background had certainly been a privileged one. Still, the fact that he'd grown up without a family or wealth hadn't seemed to bother her. She'd always had the motto that the future was what counted, not the past. And she'd had a big future planned for the both of them. Far too big to suit him.

"I don't think you could be the weepy, hand-wringing type if you tried," he said wryly.

Laurel looked away from him and out the passenger window. The snowfall was growing heavier, but she wasn't really seeing the dancing white flakes. She was seeing Lainey lying in a hospital bed, too weak to lift an arm. Laurel had openly wept at the sight of her sister and had desperately begged the doctors to do something to save her. Yet none of her emotional pleas had helped. Lainey had slipped away. And after her twin's death, a part of Laurel had frozen. She'd shut most of her feelings away, just as a way to survive, and down through the years she'd kept them locked behind a cautious heart. There had been times she'd been accused of being cold and distant. Especially by the guys she'd tried to date in the past. Laurel had found it too difficult to confide in them or explain why she'd changed from the sweet, loving girl she'd first started out to be. But in the end, that hadn't mattered. She'd not really wanted to marry any of them anyway.

She said to Russ, "I learned a long time ago that a girl with tears in her eyes can't see straight."

When he didn't make any sort of reply, she turned her head to see he was studying her with a curious eye.

"What's wrong? Why are you looking at me like that?" she asked.

"Nothing. Sometimes I just can't figure you out."

"You shouldn't try," she told him flatly. "You might hurt yourself."

He grunted with dry amusement, then changed the subject completely. "Let's stop by Burger Barn on the way out of town and pick up some sandwiches. We can eat them on the way to the ranch. Is that okay with you?"

"Sure. I'm starved."

To reach the Chaparral Ranch one had to travel west of Ruidoso, then turn north off the highway and travel several more miles on a gravel-and-dirt road to finally reach the property. Over the years, Laurel had made the trip many times to visit Alexa and her family. But once the two women had grown into adults, life had taken them in different directions and Laurel's visits to the ranch had occurred less and less often.

"Have you been out this way lately?" Russ asked as he carefully negotiated the truck around a pile of loose gravel.

They had finished eating their fast-food meal before he'd ever turned off the main highway. Which was a good thing, because recent rains had washed rough spots all over the road, making the drive worse than shaky.

His question made her wonder if he'd been reading her mind. "I've not visited the Chaparral since Alexa had her first child. She was living here at the time."

"Yeah. I remember. Her husband is a Texas Ranger. He'd come to the ranch to figure out who was doing all that cattle rustling."

Laurel nodded. "It was a scary time. The rustlers kidnapped Alexa, and if it hadn't been for Jonas they might have killed her."

"But they didn't. And all the criminals were caught and are now behind bars. So there isn't any need for you to worry that something like that might happen again."

"I'm not worried," she reasoned. "That thought never crossed my mind."

"Well, the house where you'll be living is somewhat secluded and a fair distance from the ranch yard."

"What about your house? Is it very far from mine?" she couldn't help but ask.

He thought for a moment. "Maybe a quarter mile. Is that enough distance between us?" he joked.

She laughed, but inside she told herself that she was relieved. At least she wouldn't be tempted to look out her window at night and wonder if he was home or what he was doing.

"I'm sure you'll be a good 'distant' neighbor," she told him, then cast him a curious glance. "Do you think we'll stay very busy? I understand the Chaparral runs a few thousand head of cattle and a large remuda of horses, but I figure the ranch hands take good care of all the livestock. I can't imagine too many problems cropping up."

"You know how it is with large animals. They seemed to find a way to get themselves injured. And then we'll be overseeing all the calving, foaling, vaccinating, dehorning and other routine medical programs throughout the seasons. I don't think you'll be spending a lot of time lying around on the couch peeling grapes," he told her, then cast a glance her way. "Are you feeling any better about this move?"

Moving to the Chaparral had never been the main cause of Laurel's concern. It was the hopelessness of following him, a man that would never be anything more to her than just a boss. But she could hardly tell him that. She intended for him never to know exactly what he'd come to mean to her and her life. It would ruin their working relationship and ultimately ruin her job. And she'd decided that having that much with Russ was better than having nothing with him at all.

She kept her gaze on the falling snow. "I'm not concerned now."

"What do you mean, 'now'?"

She rubbed her palms down the denim covering her thighs. "I was concerned at first, but I'm not now. That's what I mean."

"That makes a lot of sense."

She didn't know what was bringing about all this talking. Normally, Russ didn't have much to say about anything. He was usually preoccupied with his work and hardly gave her a second notice, unless she'd done something wrong, and then he would harp forever, like a dog unwilling to part with a bone. But ever since he'd told her about moving to the Chaparral, he'd made an abrupt change and was almost acting human, making Laurel wonder if he'd met a woman. What else could be softening his attitude? Maybe this other woman lived on the ranch and that's why he'd chosen to move there? That idea unsettled Laurel greatly. But she wasn't going to let herself dwell on the notion. It would be futile.

She said, "When you told me about the house—that changed everything. I haven't lived in a house since— well, since I was a teenager at home, before I left for college in Las Cruces."

From a view of his profile, she thought she saw a faint smile curve his lips and the sight surprised her. These past few days, she'd seen the man smile more than she'd ever seen him smile in her life. Yes, this change in him had to be prompted by a woman, she thought dully. She couldn't imagine him taking some sort of "nice" pill.

"Well, we're almost to the ranch, so you're just about to see this house that changed everything," he said.

About a mile before they reached the main ranch yard, Russ turned the truck onto a side road that wound upward into a thick forest full of tall pines, aspen and birch.

"I've never been on this road. Why would a house be up here?" she wanted to know.

"You'll see" was all he said.

The forest grew darker and the road steeper, until it finally turned into an S-shaped switchback. Then suddenly the forest opened up and a clearing stretched as far as Laurel could see through the falling snow.

"There's no house up here," she argued. "I think you're going to drive us off a cliff, that's what."

"You have more faith in me than that, don't you?"

Did she? The answer to that ought to be obvious. She was uprooting her home to follow him. "I did, but it's getting a little shaky," she joked.

She'd hardly gotten the remark out when a network of wooden corrals appeared, and next to them was a small barn, its red paint weathered to a pale rust color.

"Well, look at this," she murmured with surprise.

"Quint tells me they do a lot of branding and other things here. This meadow is at the bottom of a natural draw. When the cowboys drive the cattle down from the mountains, this is where the trail ends."

"Oh, I'll bet things get a little Western around here whenever roundup takes place. That might be fun."

He shot her a dry look. "Fun? Since when have you ever thought about having fun?"

For a moment his question took her aback. Did she

really come off as that stuffy, even to a man who did little more than work eighty hours a week? She didn't like to think so, but maybe the idea of her having fun was as strange to him as the notion of Russ being happy was to her.

Quickly, she unsnapped her seat belt and grabbed up her coat. As she jammed her arms into the sleeves, she said, "I've been known to laugh—once in a blue moon."

"The next time we have a blue moon, I'll remind you of that," he said.

Beyond the sweep of the headlights, a house suddenly appeared and Laurel scooted excitedly to the edge of the seat.

"Russ! It's adorable! Hurry and let me out. Is the door unlocked?"

Not waiting for his reply, she jumped out of the truck before he could get it completely parked. She ran through the snow, past a rail fence and up a walkway made of large stepping stones. When she reached the porch, she turned around to see that Russ was following, only at a much slower pace.

"Look, Russ! It has a porch with cedar posts holding up the roof. And the floor is made of planked wood, too."

He climbed the steps to join her. "So you like that, huh?"

"Are you kidding? No concrete or metal. This is all so rustic and pretty!" She turned and tried the door and was surprised to find it unlocked. "Guess they don't worry about people breaking in around here."

"I told Quint we'd be coming this evening. I'm sure he had someone unlock the houses for us. He said the keys would be left inside."

She pushed the door wide and reached inside to

search for a light switch. As soon as it flickered on, she practically leaped over the threshold and into a small entryway.

At the end of it, she stepped into a nice-size living room with a picture window that over looked the meadow and a native-rock fireplace built into one corner.

"Oh, my, a fireplace! And the room is full of furniture," she stated the obvious. "Real leather furniture! Do you think it's supposed to be here?"

Russ came to stand next to her and when she glanced up at his face, she was surprised to see that he was looking at her instead of the room. The look in his eyes was softer than she'd ever seen, sort of indulgent and kind, and the whole idea shook her even more than the excitement of seeing the house where she'd soon be living.

"Quint told me that this one was already furnished. But he says if there's something you want to change or get rid of, just let him know."

Laurel slowly shook her head in disbelief. "I never expected anything like this. I don't know what to think or say."

"Why don't we look at the rest of the rooms and see if you like them," he suggested, "before you make any decisions about the furniture."

"All right."

She turned to leave the room and was surprised when he took hold of her elbow. Sometimes during their work, they rubbed shoulders or their hands would connect. Touching him was not anything new. But having him deliberately take her arm was something totally out of the ordinary.

Don't let yourself make a big issue of it, Laurel. To-

night is different. You're both experiencing something new. He's simply being a polite escort. That's all.

The little voice inside Laurel's head should have helped her to focus on the house instead of him, but as soon as they entered the master bedroom, her eyes went straight to the queen-size mattress, and all she could think about was him and how it might be to lie next to him, to have him touch her, love her.

Oh, God, don't let her think about that now, she prayed. She didn't want him to see the longing in her eyes or to ever guess that she had any sort of feelings for him.

"I like this," she said of the varnished knotty-pine bed and accompanying chest and dresser. Leaving his side, she walked over and ran a hand over the Native American blanket covering the mattress. "Everything looks so Western. I'm actually going to feel like I'm living on a ranch."

"You will be living on a ranch."

She dared to look at him and was surprised to feel her breathing had quickened, along with her heartbeat. What was this place doing to her? she wondered. She'd spent hours and hours alone with this man for the past five years. This was nothing new. Just because the two of them were together in a secluded house didn't change the fact that they were, at the most, friends.

Glancing away from him, she walked over to an eight-drawer chest. Atop it stood a small lamp with different ranch brands printed on the beige-fabric shade. She absently touched the edge of it, as she asked, "I wonder who used to live in this place?"

"I think it was the cook's elderly mother. She passed away a few months ago."

"You must mean Reena's mother, Tiwa," Laurel said.

"I used to see the old woman when I visited the ranch. She'd be in the kitchen with her daughter. But after she began to age, I didn't see her much. I believe she was close to a hundred when she died. I wonder why the Cantrells provided her with such nice housing."

He shrugged. "I couldn't say. But I'm betting the old woman probably worked for them in her younger days."

"Hmm. I'll have to ask Alexa the next time I speak with her." She moved away from the chest and started toward the door. "Let's look at the rest of the place."

He followed her out of the bedroom and across a short hallway to a second bedroom. It was smaller, but still a good size. The bathroom was jammed between the two bedrooms, and directly behind the living room was the kitchen.

As soon as they walked into the kitchen, Laurel spotted a note on the table and she quickly scooped it up and began to read out loud: "'Laurel, I've cleaned up most of the dust and laundered the bedding. If there's anything else you need or want, just let us know at the big house. Welcome! Sassy.'"

"Do you know Sassy?" Russ asked.

"Yes. She's the housekeeper at the big house. I'll have to thank her for all the cleaning." She lowered the note, then looked at him and shook her head with amazement. "Russ, when you said I would be getting housing with the job, I thought at best it would be manufactured. But this—it's like a little mansion to me!"

He walked over to where she stood beside the table, and the faint grin on his lips made her groan inside. He didn't have a clue that he was shamefully sexy. Nor did he have a clue that she would love to wrap her body around his, to feel his whiskered cheek rub against her skin, his lips tasting hers.

"Then you're happy about this?" he asked.

She gave her head a mental shake, while hoping her cheeks weren't as pink as they felt. "If you're talking about the house and furniture, then yes, I'm very, very happy. If you're talking about the job, well, I can't answer that until we start working."

A little scowl drew his brows together. "What if you don't like it?"

She shrugged as she met his gaze. "What if you don't like it?" she retorted.

One corner of his mouth crooked upward. "Touché."

Swallowing at the ball of nerves in her throat, she moved around him and walked over to the cabinets. As she pretended to inspect the stainless-steel sink, she told herself that she had to get a grip. Nothing had really changed between them. Something about this place only made it feel that way.

She heard his footsteps approaching from behind and then suddenly she felt his hand rest on her shoulder. For a moment she practically stopped breathing and her eyes instinctively closed as she tried to brace herself.

"Laurel, I think I should apologize."

His words stunned her completely and she forgot that he was standing so close until she whirled around to face him. And suddenly she realized her breasts were very nearly brushing his chest, and his face was only inches from hers.

"Apologize?" she asked quietly. "For what?"

He grimaced. "I don't know—just seeing you here tonight—it's made me realize that I was asking far more of you than I had a right to."

"You let me make my own decision," she said in a voice that sounded breathy, even to her ears. "No one twisted my arm to be here."

"No. But you liked the clinic and you've always lived in town. I'm asking you to make some huge changes. And you said you didn't like change."

He remembered her saying that? Maybe she'd better keep a closer watch on what she was saying to this man.

"I did say that," she agreed. "But sometimes a person's life needs to be shaken a little, just to keep things interesting. Besides, you needn't worry about me. You have far more things of your own to deal with."

He let out a heavy breath, then lifted his cowboy hat and ran a hand through his tousled hair. "You're really too good for me."

In an effort to lighten the moment, she quietly laughed. "I know that."

His brown eyes locked with hers as his body moved ever so much closer to hers. "You're laughing," he pointed out in a low voice. "And it's not a blue moon."

"No," she said inanely, while wondering wildly what he was doing and why. He'd never looked at her this way. Never touched her this way. "Sometimes it just slips out of me."

He let out another long breath, and Laurel could feel the warmth of it brushing her cheeks. Thankfully, she had a scarf wrapped around her neck; otherwise he'd be able to see the pulse pounding rapidly at the base of her throat.

"I'm glad you can laugh, Laurel. I'm glad you're happy with the house. And I'm glad you chose to come here with me."

His words were buzzing through her brain, even as she watched his lips growing closer and closer to hers.

Was he actually going to kiss her?

The incredulous thought had barely skipped through

her head when his palm came up to rest against her cheek and his lips came down on hers.

For a brief second as their lips made contact, she was sure her heart stopped completely. And then suddenly every part of her body was flooded with sensations so intense she staggered back slightly against the cabinet counter.

He moved with her, and for what seemed like an eternity, but not nearly long enough, his lips moved over hers in a warm, thorough search that sucked every ounce of breath from her body.

When he finally lifted his head and broke the contact between them, Laurel was visibly shaken, and she stared at him as fear came rushing in behind a wall of desire.

"What— Why did you do that?" she finally managed to ask.

Regret, or something like it, twisted his features. "I don't know. I'm sorry."

"I don't want to hear that from you."

"All right. You won't," he retorted, his demeanor suddenly changing back to the boss she'd dealt with for the past five fears.

With a tiny groan, she twisted away from him and hurried out of the kitchen. He followed her into the living room, but stopped a few feet away from where she stood near the picture window.

Glancing over her shoulder, her gaze slid over him, his stance wide and his hands thrust deep into the pockets of his coat. Although there was nothing inviting about the expression on his face, Laurel still wanted to run and fling her arms around him.

She was crazy, she thought. Hopelessly crazy.

"If you've seen enough, I think we'd better be heading on to the other house," he suggested gruffly.

Laurel looked out the window and wondered why now, after all this time, she felt tears burning her throat and stinging the backs of her eyes. Since Lainey had died, she rarely ever shed tears over anything. It wasn't right that Russ could pull that much emotion from her.

She said stiffly, "If you don't mind, I'd rather stay here and look at things a bit more."

"All right. I'll be back in a few minutes," he told her.

She nodded and he quickly left the house. From her spot at the window, she watched his headlights pull away, then head on up the mountain. But once they were completely out of sight, she sank weakly onto the arm of the couch and dropped her head in her hands.

This wasn't going to work, she thought sickly. Not this lovely little house, or the job, or him. Because his kiss had shown her exactly how much she was missing and all the things she could never have. Wherever she went on this ranch he'd be nearby and his kiss would be haunting her, tempting her. How could she ever endure that much misery?

She'd have to bear it, she told herself. Or live her life without him. And that was a choice she wasn't quite ready to make.

Chapter Four

By the time Russ returned a half hour later, Laurel had managed to compose herself somewhat and was determined to act as though nothing had happened between her and her boss.

But the moment she climbed into the truck and they pulled away from the house, Russ said, "That kiss—I honestly don't know what came over me, Laurel. You were—well, it was nice to see you smile and hear you laugh. It's been a big relief to me that you've agreed to continue working as my assistant, and I guess I got carried away for a moment."

"That's all?" she asked stiffly, wondering why his explanation left her feeling strangely deflated.

"That's all. So I think we should both forget it. Don't you?"

Forcing herself to glance his way, she saw that he was focused on the dirt road in front of them and his profile gave none of his feelings away. But that was hardly a surprise. The only times she'd ever seen Russ show much emotion were when they were treating animals that had been deliberately hurt or neglected. When it came to people, he appeared to not feel much at all.

So why had she felt so, so much in his kiss? she wondered.

Swallowing at the thickness in her throat, she turned her attention to the passenger window. Even the darkness couldn't hide the heavy snowfall that was already collecting on the tree branches and ground vegetation near the edge of the road.

"Consider it forgotten," she said, then cleared her throat to ease the huskiness in her voice. "What did you think of your house?"

"It was fine. It has everything I need." He paused for a moment before adding, "I've hired a moving van to bring my things out on Thursday. If you'd like to have your things hauled with mine, I'll send the movers by your place."

"Will there be enough room for my stuff on the truck, too?" she asked, while she tried her best to focus on the necessary things she had to do in the next few days. But that was hard to do when her mind kept reliving the feel of his lips on hers, the touch of his hand on her face. She'd told him she would forget their kiss, but how did a person go about forgetting their hopes and dreams, their deepest longings?

"Plenty. I'm downsizing on furniture and lots of other belongings. In fact, I've already scheduled a charity to pick up a load of things that I don't need or want to bring with me."

"Oh. In that case, I'll take you up on the offer. It'll

be just as easy to pay you as it would be for me to hire a mover for my stuff."

"I won't accept any pay from you," he said gruffly. "Consider it a job perk. I'm the cause of this move, so the expense should be on me."

Russ had always been a generous boss. Not only did he pay her a hefty salary, he also included nice benefits with it. But the earnings she made were not what kept her by his side, and sometimes she wondered if he realized that.

"In that case, I'll accept your offer."

He briefly glanced her way and then, turning his attention back to the road, shook his head. "You don't like to accept help from anyone, do you?"

Surprised by his question, she studied his profile. "I don't like to be beholden to anyone."

"Why? Afraid they might ask something of you that you can't give?"

She frowned at him. "That's a strange question. You make it sound like I don't like people. Period."

"Sometimes I don't believe you do. Animals, yes." he conceded. "But not people."

His remark took her aback, and she turned her face toward the window so he couldn't see how much it had affected her. "I can't imagine why you would think such a thing," she said lowly.

Because you don't encourage anyone to get close to you, Russ wanted to say, but stopped himself short. He'd already gotten personal enough with her tonight. In fact, he didn't know what in hell had come over him back there in Laurel's house. The two of them had been discussing the rooms and furnishings, and then suddenly, without even realizing it, he'd found himself standing close to her, and she'd looked so warm and pretty, her lips so inviting.

With a mental shake of his head, he once again tried to push the thoughts of kissing her out of his mind, but each time he shoved, they came right back to torment him. He'd never expected her to taste so sweet, or that kissing her would feel so perfect, and he was far more shaken than he wanted to admit.

"You're not a people person, Laurel. That's all I'm trying to say." He glanced over to see she was still staring out the passenger window. Yet even if she'd been looking directly at him, he doubted he could have read her thoughts. "Have you ever had a boyfriend?"

That brought her head around with a jerk, and as she stared at him in wonder, his gaze dropped to her parted lips.

"Don't you think that question should have come before the kiss?"

Russ felt a blush creeping over his face, and he thought he must be an idiot for ever letting the question slip out in the first place.

"Probably," he admitted. "But it wouldn't hurt you to answer anyway."

She looked away from him and stared straight on. "Yes. I've had boyfriends in the past. Not recently."

"Why not recently?"

"I don't know any man who's worth the time."

"Oh."

She darted a glance at him. "Have you had any girlfriends lately?"

Her question caused a caustic laugh to slip past his lips. No, but he had a pregnant ex-wife. "No," he said gruffly. "I barely have time to have a conversation with Leo, much less a woman."

"Would you like to have a woman in your life?"

He'd just accused her of being distant when it came to her personal life; now she was asking him a *very* private question. Maybe he didn't understand anything about women, he thought. He'd evidently gotten things wrong about Brooke. Now Laurel was proving he didn't really know her, either.

"Yes. The right woman," he admitted. "To share things and grow old with."

She sighed. "I suppose I've gotten accustomed to living alone."

"I think I remember Maccoy saying that your father and brother moved away from Lincoln County several years ago. You didn't want to go with them?"

One of her shoulders lifted and fell as though she was indifferent to the whole matter. But when she spoke, her voice sounded unusually raspy, as if she was pushing the words through a throat full of nails.

"Not really. This is where I was born and grew up. It's my home. Besides, I wasn't invited."

Russ stared at the snowy road in front of them while her last words rolled through his head. "Why not? You don't get along with your relatives?"

"I get along with them. They just choose not to live close to me. Nor me to them."

"I don't understand. You say you get along with them, yet you make it sound like there's a rift between you."

She released a long sigh, then turned slightly in the seat toward him. When Russ spared a glance at her, he almost wished he'd kept his mouth shut and not asked her anything. Even in the dim lighting of the cab, he could tell she'd gone pale and there was a tautness to her features that could only stem from hurt and anger.

"Since you seemed to want to know about my family life, I'll explain, Russ. My family finds it difficult to be around me. I remind them of disease and dying and their own uselessness."

Laurel's twin sister had died in her early teens, he thought. If not for Maccoy, even this fact would have been unknown to him. And the old man only knew about the tragedy because he'd lived in the same community as the Stantons at the time the girl had died. Laurel certainly hadn't told Maccoy or Russ about it. But she was mentioning the subject now, and seeing the pain on her face made him feel like a bastard for questioning her in the first place. It was none of his business what went on between Laurel and her family. Yet he wanted to know what made this private woman tick, what made her live only to work and do nothing more.

"Maccoy told me about your sister. Not long after you came to work at the clinic," he admitted. "I never mentioned it because—well, we never talk about such things."

Her head bent slightly. "No," she agreed. "And talking about Lainey is still very hard for me."

Maybe that was because she'd never talked enough about her, Russ thought. Maybe if she had, she'd be better able to deal with the matter now. But he wasn't about to push her tonight. He'd already upset her enough with that damned kiss.

"Well, I don't expect you to talk to me about your sister. But I will say one thing—I think it's awful that your family finds it painful to be around you. Seems to me that you'd be a comfort to them."

She darted a glance at him, and he turned his head in time to see a grateful little smile touch her lips. The sight surprised him completely.

"Thank you for saying that, Russ," she murmured.

"But it's okay that they're not here. To be frank, it's just as upsetting for me to be around them."

"I see." By now they were entering the outskirts of Ruidoso and the traffic was growing heavier. Russ was forced to keep his eyes on the taillights in front of him. "Well, my parents are both dead," he said. "Or I should say, my mother is dead. As for my old man, I have no idea, so I consider him dead to me."

"Oh," she said in a small voice. "I didn't know."

He released a heavy breath. "It's something I don't talk about, either."

She didn't say anything to that, and the two of them remained silent until they returned to the clinic. Once he'd parked his truck next to hers, she quickly jerked the door open and slid to the ground. By the time Russ joined her, she had already opened the door of her own vehicle. But instead of climbing in, she turned and spoke to him.

"Thank you for showing me the house," she said stiffly.

"You're welcome." Awkward tension stretched between them like a piece of prickly barbed wire, and whether he'd intended it or not, it was clear that kissing her tonight had changed everything between them. "I'm glad you liked it."

The lighting behind the clinic was dim, but still bright enough for him to see her gaze drop to the ground. For some reason he didn't understand, he wanted to take her into his arms, stroke her hair and assure her that everything was going to be all right.

She said, "It's been twelve years or more since I've lived in a house. I was eighteen at the time and the house belonged to my father. After I graduated high school, I moved out and into a college dorm, and since then a string of apartments have been home to me." Her head swung back and forth. "This is going to be different for me, Russ. Very different."

The faint sadness in her voice had him wrapping a comforting hand around her upper arm. "It's going to be different for me, too, Laurel. We'll be making this change together."

She lifted her face, and he couldn't help but notice a quiver to her lips. And though there were snowflakes falling between them, he didn't think the vulnerable reaction was caused by the cold air.

"Russ, that kiss—I think I ought to tell you that it was…nice."

This was the last thing he'd expected to hear from her, and for long moments he was too stunned to speak. Finally, he said, "I told you to forget it."

"Yes, you did. But I—well, I'm a bit ashamed of the way I reacted so coldly about it all."

Cold? There'd been nothing cold about her kiss. In fact, it had felt red-hot to him. Even now, just thinking of it heated his insides and made him forget the freezing wind blowing between their faces.

"You didn't," he said.

"Maybe not. But I'm— I guess what I'm trying to say is that it's been a long time since I've been that close to a man. And the truth is I'm not very experienced with such things. It caught me off guard, that's all."

"You don't have to explain, Laurel," he said softly. "We were both caught off guard. So let's just call it a celebration kiss for our new jobs, okay?"

She nodded in agreement, but he could see there was still a slight tremble to her lips, and everything inside Russ wanted to kiss it away. The notion stunned him. He'd worked at this woman's side for more than five years. Why had it taken him so long to see her as a woman? And what was this going to do to their working relationship? To him?

"Sure," she said. "I can do that."

He squeezed her arm. "Good. Now, both of us better get out of this weather. See you in the morning."

"Yes. In the morning," she echoed.

He helped her into the cab of her truck, and after quickly starting the engine, she pulled away from the building. Once she was out of sight, Russ ignored his own vehicle and quickly let himself in the back of the clinic. He didn't want to go home just yet. He didn't want to be reminded of his broken, childless marriage. Nor did he want to sit around and try to figure out what had occurred between him and Laurel tonight. Work had always been a cure for what ailed him, and he had plenty to do before he turned over the clinic at the end of the week.

For the next three days, Laurel remained at a run as she worked a full day at the clinic and got her belongings packed for the moving truck. Not to mention dealing with utility companies and her apartment lease, which by luck would be ending in the next few days anyway.

She'd had little time to sit and dwell on the kiss she'd shared with Russ last Tuesday night. For the most part, she'd tried to do as he'd suggested and forget it. But that was like asking a person to forget to breathe. The memory of those moments, of his lips caressing and tasting hers, continued to haunt her, especially when she was in his presence. And she realized that she would never be able to go back to seeing him simply as her boss.

Who are you kidding, Laurel? You've always looked at Russ as more than a boss. You see him as a man. A

*man who makes your heart race, your body yearn to be
loved in every way a woman wants to be loved.*

Trying to shut her ears to the taunting voice in her
head, Laurel quickly strode to the front of the clinic,
where Maccoy was busy packing away files and papers
that Russ intended to take with him.

The older man was kneeling on the floor, cleaning
out the bottom drawer of a metal cabinet, when Laurel entered the room. He looked around, then cocked a
questioning brow at her.

"Need something, Lauralee?" he asked, using the
nickname he'd hung on her the very first day they'd met
more than five years ago.

Maccoy was five foot six at the most and barely carried enough fat to cover his bones. But he was as strong
as an ox and never seemed to run out of energy. His
sparse hair was a mix of red and gray, and Laurel figured at one time in his youth he'd been a fiery carrottop
with a personality to match. Now his face was terribly
wrinkled and weather-beaten, but most of it was usually
dusted with a layer of rust-red, day-old whiskers. As for
his personality, the gruffness of his voice couldn't hide
the enormous size of his heart.

"Nope. Just wanted to let you know I'll be gone for
a couple of hours. The movers are ready to load my
things, and I need to be at the apartment to make sure
they get what I want to take with me and leave behind
what I don't want."

He shot her a smug grin. "I moved all my stuff yesterday evening. In fact, I'm gonna spend my first night
in the bunkhouse with the boys tonight."

Laurel smiled at him while wishing she felt as chip-
per about this move as Maccoy did. "You sound happy
about it."

"Why the hell not? This new job is gonna be like walking down easy street compared to this workhouse," he said frankly.

Shortly after Laurel had started working at Hollister Animal Clinic, it had been easy to see that Maccoy was the wheel that kept the spokes of the outfit held together. He kept everything in order, including hysterical and demanding pet owners.

"No one works harder than you do around here, Maccoy. I'm glad a load is going to be lifted from your shoulders."

A wry grin twisted up one corner of his lips. "I'm gonna have company, too. My darlin' Mae died more than fifteen years ago, and I've been by myself ever since. It'll be nice to have a person to talk to or have a game of cards with once in a while."

"I'm happy to hear you're looking forward to it," she told him, while thinking she was a lot like Maccoy. She'd been left on her own for a long time now, and after a while she'd gotten used to it, but that didn't mean she necessarily liked living a solitary life. She just didn't know how to go about changing it without taking a major risk, one that might open her up to a world of hurt.

Rising to his feet, the old man lifted one of the boxes from the floor and placed it on a nearby desk. "Well, the happiest part about all this is Russ. I've been praying he'd realize he needed to let up and get a life. And he's finally doing it."

With a thoughtful tilt to her head, she looked at the elderly man as he shuffled through a stack of files. "Maccoy, what do you think caused Russ to make this move? To be honest, the news knocked me for a loop. I wouldn't have guessed he had anything like this on his mind."

"Hmm. Well, Russ keeps his feelings pretty much to himself. But I'd say he finally figured out that he was plain ole tired. And he's figured out, too, that he's made a boatload of money over the years and it hasn't made him happy. Put those two things together and it probably wasn't hard for him to see he needed to get the hell out of Dodge."

Russ was not a wishy-washy man. He was stable, methodical and confident about his work, Laurel thought. Each task he performed was done with precision, and his focus remained on a steady, straightforward course until it was completed. He was a man who rarely made changes. Unless he thought they were needed. The fact that he'd never replaced her or Maccoy was proof of that.

"Maybe so. I just have a feeling there was more to his decision than that. But I suppose it doesn't matter now. We're all headed to the Chaparral. Let's hope it was the right thing to do—for all of us."

With a shake of his head, he walked over and curled an arm around Laurel's shoulders. "You've always worried too much, Lauralee. You need to look at life like ridin' a bronc. The moment you start gettin' scared and stiff, that's the split second you're gonna fall off."

Laurel couldn't help but chuckle and she leaned over and kissed his grizzled cheek. "I'll try to remember that, Maccoy. Right now I'd better be going."

Later that night, Laurel stood in the middle of her new living room and marveled at all the space that still remained around her even after the moving men had hauled in her television, two wooden rockers, several lamps, potted plants and a magazine rack.

Moving into her beautiful little house had taken away some of the sting of leaving the familiar confines of the clinic back in town. And as she moved around the rooms, singing along with the radio, unpacking boxes and placing items where she wanted them to be, she decided that Maccoy was right. She needed to quit worrying so much and start enjoying.

But being fearful and anxious were traits she'd developed long ago, when she'd first learned that her sister was ill. At ten years old, most healthy children didn't dwell on death or dying. Laurel certainly hadn't. She and Lainey had both been carefree, bubbly girls who found more reasons to laugh than cry. But in a matter of days, Lainey had gone from feeling tired to being diagnosed with a serious blood disease. And from that moment on, Laurel had learned just how fragile and changeable life could be.

After her sister's diagnosis, Laurel had pretty much gone from fun-loving child to nursemaid and constant companion to her ailing sister. As a result, she'd lost friendships, missed important milestones and been forced to grow up overnight. And each time Lainey's health had deteriorated to a new low, Laurel's usually sunny optimism had sunk, until one day it disappeared completely.

Now, years after the loss of her sister, Laurel struggled to instill herself with any sort of hope. Most of the time, she expected the worst, so that when the worst came, she'd be prepared. She knew it was not a pretty outlook for anyone to have, yet she didn't know how to break out of the darkness that surrounded her.

She was placing a stack of folded clothes into a dresser drawer when she heard a faint knock on the front door. Surprised that anyone would be stopping by on this cold night, she hurried through the house.

Russ was the last person she expected to see when she opened the door. But there he was, standing in the middle of the porch, bundled in a heavy parka, a large brown bag tucked beneath one arm.

He grinned at her faintly. "May I come in?"

Her heart beating fast, she pushed the door wider. "Certainly."

"The movers just left my place," he said as he followed her into the house. "I thought I'd eat before I started unpacking, and I have plenty for two. I took a chance that you'd still be here and drove down."

She'd not seen Russ since earlier this afternoon, before she'd left the clinic to deal with the moving van. He'd not mentioned anything about stopping by, and the idea that he wanted to share his meal with her was more than surprising. There'd been times in the past when he'd done something thoughtful for her, like an extra bonus on her check for no particular reason, or paying the cost of the movers as he had today. But he'd never done anything this personal, and she could only wonder why he was doing it now.

"I decided I might as well stay here tonight," she said as she walked toward the kitchen. "There's nothing left at my apartment, except a bed without linens and a bare refrigerator and cupboards. Besides, we only have one more day left at the clinic. I don't mind making the drive in the morning."

"No need for that. I'll stop by and pick you up," he told her as he placed the sack on the pine tabletop.

Turning, she looked at him. "Oh. You're staying here on the ranch tonight, too?"

He nodded. "My house back in town is stripped of everything, even furniture. I don't think I'd get much rest sleeping on a hard floor."

So tonight he would be staying in his house, which was a short distance up the mountain from her, she thought. From now on when the two of them weren't working, they would be close neighbors. The idea filled her with a strange mixture of unease and excitement.

"I doubt it," she agreed, then turned back to the cabinet counter where a stack of dishes still sat in a heavy cardboard box. "Do we need plates?"

"There's paper ones with the food. I can eat off anything," he told her.

She collected the plates and utensils to go with them, while he pulled the containers of food from the sack.

"I have to confess, I wasn't smart enough to think about stopping and getting anything to eat before I drove out here," he said. "Reena was kind enough to send this out to me."

As she joined him at the table, a whiff of fried chicken caused her mouth to water. "That was very thoughtful of her."

"Yeah. One of the ranch hands delivered it a few minutes ago. It appears they want us to feel welcome," he said. "And I appreciate that."

"So do I," she agreed as she placed one plate at the end of the table for him and another at the side for her. "I'm not sure I have any soda for drinks. But we can always have water or coffee."

"Reena sent a thermos of something to drink, too," he said as he reached into the sack and pulled out a small red-and-white insulated thermos with a handle on the top. "I think it's full of iced tea. There's also salt, pepper and hot sauce in the sack."

"The woman thought of everything," Laurel said with amazement. "I'll be sure to thank her when I'm over at the big house."

She gestured for him to take a seat at the end of the

table. "Sit down and I'll see if I can find the boxes with my glassware."

Once she returned with the glasses and was seated kitty-corner to his right, Russ poured their drinks and they began to fill their plates with the food Reena had so graciously supplied.

"Did you bring Leo with you tonight?" she asked as she ladled baked beans on her plate.

"Yes. And he's pretty angry with me right now, because I made him ride out here in a cat carrier."

Laurel chuckled. "What else would a cat ride in?"

"Oh, he thinks he's above that. He wants to sit on the truck seat, like a dog. When you found that stray, you found one of a kind," he said with wry fondness. "What about your dogs and cats?"

"The dogs are out back in their doghouse, and the cats are here in the house somewhere. They were terrified. All three made a dash beneath the bed."

"They'll get used to their new surroundings," he assured her. "We all will with time."

She looked at him, her gaze slowly wandering over his rugged face. The rusty-brown whiskers that covered his jaws and circled his lips were even longer than usual, and faint lines of fatigue were etched beneath his eyes. His sandy-blond hair curled ever so slightly around his ears, and the top looked as though he'd finger combed it to one side in order to keep the thick hank of fringe out of his eyes. His appearance was nothing close to being groomed, she thought, yet he was a delicious sight. One that reminded her she was hungry for more than just the food on her plate.

Forcing her gaze back to her plate, she tried to keep the memory of his kiss at bay. "We haven't actually had time to discuss this, but when exactly did you plan to start work here on the ranch?"

"Not officially until Monday. But I plan to drive over to the ranch yard on Saturday morning and look over the facilities. Quint has gone to great pains to create a regular animal hospital for us. Would you like to go along? I thought you might be anxious to see it, too."

Why did it seem as if they were suddenly doing so much more together as a pair? she wondered. Nothing had really changed in that aspect. She and Russ had worked and traveled together all over Lincoln County and beyond. They'd spent hours and hours alone together, and though she'd always found him attractive, she'd never before been consumed with this new sexual tension that had sprung up between them. She'd never been so aware of being a female as she was now—now that he'd given her that kiss.

Oh, God, this was going to be so hard, she thought. But hard or not, she had to forget. She had to remember they were working partners and nothing more.

"Sure, I'd like to tag along," she said as casually as she could. "I'm eager to see our new work area. Even before we look at everything, I can tell you that Quint has provided you with the best medicine and equipment. That's just the type of people the Cantrells are. But there is something that's been bothering me a bit about this whole thing."

He looked over at her, a faint crease marring his forehead. "What is that?" he wanted to know.

"I'm going to miss treating all the small animals that passed through the clinic in town. From now on, we'll be working on cattle and horses, calves and foals. I'm going to miss the cats and dogs and bunnies and birds and all the other furry and feathered creatures we cared for."

His features softened with understanding. "I'm sure there will be pets on the ranch that will need vet services," he told her, then added with a suggestive grin, "and you can always give Leo his vaccines and parasite treatments."

Laurel suddenly laughed, because they both had experienced the black cat's horrible attitude about taking shots and pills. "Thanks, Russ. But I don't think I'll miss small animal care *that* much."

He laughed along with her and the easy exchange allowed Laurel to relax. For the next few minutes, she was able to enjoy the food on her plate while they discussed some of the bigger projects they'd be dealing with come spring, when both calves and foals began to drop.

After they finished eating their share of chicken and accompanying vegetables, she made coffee to go with the slices of chocolate cake that the Chaparral cook had provided for dessert. As Laurel stood at the cabinet counter waiting for the brewing to finish, she suggested, "I suppose we could take our dessert out to the living room and eat it in front of the fireplace. There isn't a fire, but we could pretend."

"Why pretend?" he said as he rose to his feet. "There's a stack of firewood on the front porch. I'll build one for you."

"Would you?" she asked gratefully. "I've never had a fireplace. I don't know the first thing about building a fire. Now that I'm living out here, I need to learn."

"Then we'll need a bit of paper and a box of matches. Think you can find those things while I carry in the wood?" he asked.

"No problem," she told him. "I'll meet you in the living room."

Short minutes later, Russ knelt before the native-rock hearth and motioned for Laurel to join him. "First of all, you need to learn how to stack everything," he said as she eased down close to his side. "Crumple the paper and place it on the grates first, then the kindling."

"Exactly what is this kindling you're using?" she asked as she laid the paper across the iron grates. "It looks different from sticks of firewood."

"That's because it is different. It's chopped pieces of seasoned pine, like old pine knots or logs that have died and turned hard. It makes a quick, hot flame because it's full of resin."

Just as he'd started a sudden, hot flame in her that night he'd kissed her, she thought. She'd never felt such an instant jolt of sensations in her life. Had he felt it, too? she wondered. No. He'd been a married man once. He knew all about kissing and making love and experiencing passions of the flesh. Whereas she'd had very little experience with the opposite sex.

Clearing her throat, she asked, "Will I always need kindling to start a fire?"

"If you start it from scratch, you will." He crossed several sticks of firewood over the kindling, then stuck a lighted match to the paper. The tiny flame quickly grew as it reached the pine, then licked its way up the small logs. "But the forest around here is full of pine. I'll keep it chopped for you."

"Oooh, that already feels good and warm," she said as she sat back on her haunches and shoved her open palms toward the growing flames. "This is going to be nice. Coming home to a fire after a cold day at work."

He turned his head to look at her, and as Laurel met his gaze, her breath caught in her throat. The warm glint in his eyes was not a reflection of the hot flames. No, it was that same look she'd seen that night he'd kissed her. She'd never expected to see it again, and suddenly her heart was thudding rapidly.

"Yes," he murmured. "It will be nice."

Every womanly particle inside her wanted to lean into him. She wanted to relive the experience of his lips against hers, moving, tasting, teasing. She wanted to rest her hands upon his shoulders and feel the hard strength of his muscles. She wanted—

Determined not to let desire take a total grip on her senses, she mentally shook herself and started to rise. "Uh—I think—the fire is going," she said, her voice oddly hoarse. "I'll go get the coffee and cake."

Halfway to her feet, Russ caught her by the hand and tugged her back down on the braided rug. The momentum caused her to fall sideways, but rather than steadying her to an upright position, he pulled her directly into his arms.

"Forget the cake and coffee," he ordered under his breath.

Her eyes wide, she unwittingly wedged her palms between his chest and hers as though that was enough to deter any further contact between them. "Russ— what—"

"I was a fool for saying we should forget that kiss, Laurel. I've been a fool for waiting this long to kiss you again."

Her gasp of surprise was suddenly swallowed up as he fastened his mouth hungrily over hers, and with a tiny whimper of surrender, she closed her eyes and let the flood of sensations sweep her away.

Chapter Five

Russ didn't know how long he continued to kiss Laurel. Nor did he realize that the two of them had listed sideways and onto the braided rug. The where or why didn't matter. Nothing mattered except having her soft lips beneath his, her warm body pressed against him.

But eventually, he felt her small hands pushing at his shoulders, her lips pulling back from his, and the realization that she wanted to end the kiss finally registered in his fuzzy brain. Slowly, he lifted his head to gaze down at her, and the sight of her pink, puffy lips had him groaning with desire.

"I've been wanting to do that again ever since I kissed you the other night," he confessed, as his hands gently kneaded the flesh covering her shoulder blades.

A rosy color spread across her cheeks, and Russ wondered if she'd never had a man speak such things to her. She didn't kiss as though she was entirely inexperienced, yet there was a shyness about her that said she wasn't accustomed to being in a man's embrace.

"Is that why you brought the meal down here to eat with me?" she asked, her low voice faintly accusing. "You had this planned?"

He smiled at her. "You know me well enough to know that I'm not a calculating man."

Her gray gaze slowly searched his face. "You're not an impulsive one, either. So maybe you should explain what this is all about."

Her question didn't surprise him. It was only natural for her to wonder about this sudden change in his behavior, yet that didn't make him any more prepared to give her an answer.

Raking a hand through his tumbled hair, he eased away from her and rose to his feet. She quickly followed and stood only inches away, facing him, waiting for him to speak. But in all truth, Russ wasn't in the mood to talk. For the first time in years, he wanted to make love to a woman and he didn't want anything to interrupt the feeling, the hot desire that had been lost to him for so long.

"I can't explain, Laurel. If I said I could, I'd be lying," he said honestly.

She looked at him for a moment longer, then with a frustrated groan, she turned her back to him. "You're ruining everything, Russ. All these years we've worked so well together. And now we'll never be able to go back to what we had. I hate you for that. Really hate you."

"Laurel! How could you say something like that?" Moving closer, he wrapped his hands over the tops of her shoulders. She wasn't a fragile woman. She was tall and strong with just the right amount of fleshy curves, and yet she felt so delicate and vulnerable. And he suddenly realized just how much he wanted to protect her, to keep her happy and safe.

"You just kissed me like you wanted to kiss me. Not like you hated me for doing it," he gently reasoned.

With her back still to him, she bent her head as though she was in agony, and to Russ the hopeless reaction was almost as bad as a slap in the face.

"That's true," she said in a ragged voice. "I did want to. But the whole thing is—not good."

With his hands still on her shoulders, he forced her to turn and face him. "Maybe you should explain what that means," he said.

Glancing away from him, she let out a helpless moan. "It means—" She paused long enough to swallow. "I don't want to have an affair with you."

"Did I ask you to have an affair?"

Her face jerked back to his and he could see his question had embarrassed her. A deep, bright red splotched her cheeks and throat.

"No. But—" She stopped, pressed her lips together, then shook her head. "I realize I sound silly and naive. I know I'm inexperienced with men and going at this all wrong. But I don't know how else to say it. I don't want us to have a—personal relationship of any kind."

"Why?"

That brought her head back around to his, and this time he could see pain in the depths of her eyes, a desolate look that he couldn't understand or accept.

"Because it would be a mistake. We'd end up hurting each other. And I don't think either of us wants that."

"How could you be so certain it wouldn't work? You have a glass ball that gives you a view of the future? If you do, you'd better throw it away. We're not supposed to know what's in store for us—we wouldn't really be living that way—we'd be robots."

She sighed, and though Russ had heard her sigh many times before in the past, this sound was different. It came from deep within, and the heavy weight of defeat it carried actually stunned him.

"You don't understand, Russ."

Suddenly he was more than a little annoyed with her; he was downright angry. "You couldn't be more right, Laurel! I can't understand how a young, beautiful and healthy woman like you could feel so negative, so sorry for yourself."

She squirmed away from him, and he watched her walk over to the picture window and stare at the blackness beyond the thick plate of glass.

"That's not true!" she muttered.

"Isn't it?"

"No!"

He quickly strode over to where she stood and circled his hand around her upper arm. "You told me the other night that no man was worth wasting your time over. Is that the way you feel about me? I thought— We've been together for a long time now, Laurel. And I'd be the first to admit that we quarrel and sometimes we even yell at each other. But I've always felt like you respected me, even liked me. Have I been wrong all this time?"

Still facing the window, she shook her head. "No. You're not wrong. I do like and respect you, Russ. I always have. That's why I don't want us to ruin everything between us."

"Why would us getting closer ruin things? It could make them nicer—much nicer," he said gently.

Once again her head wagged back and forth in a defeated motion. "I'm not cut out to be any man's wife or girlfriend. I wouldn't know how to be."

Before he could ask her to explain such a perplexing statement, it suddenly dawned on him that fear had been laced through her voice. The idea stopped him short, and as he studied the back of her bent head, he realized that he'd always understood that Laurel was different from any woman he'd ever known. He just hadn't recognized how different.

"I don't know where that sort of thinking is coming from," he said tenderly, "and I'm not going to ask you to explain any of it tonight. But I will tell you this. As far as I'm concerned, things are just getting started between us and you might as well get ready to deal with it— with me."

Whirling around to him, she stared, her lips parted with surprise. "You say you don't understand me, Russ. Well, I can say the same about you! Why this sudden personal interest in me? You've never given me a second look as a woman before. Why now? Now that you've sold the clinic and we've moved out here?"

Even if he'd wanted to rationalize his behavior to her, he couldn't. He only knew that something had happened to him that day he'd spotted Brooke dining with her friends. Suddenly snapshots of himself, his life and work began to preoccupy his thoughts. At thirty-eight he wasn't an old man by any stretch of the imagination, yet he was past the age where most men had settled into a family life with a wife and children.

Russ had been an only child and once his mother died, the only relatives left were a few distant cousins he'd never met and an uncle who had not supplied him with any sense of family connection. The loneliness of his childhood had molded Russ's outlook on everything, and by the time he'd grown into a teenager, he'd vowed to have himself a big family. He would love them and they would love him back and he'd never be alone. But building a veterinary business and the failure of his marriage had gotten in the way of his dreams.

Seeing Brooke pregnant had reminded him that he was still stuck in the same rut, still working eighty or ninety hours a week and going home to an empty house. Brooke had moved on and she was noticeably happier for it. The fact had opened his eyes wide and clear, and he'd started seeing everything in a new light. Especially Laurel.

Reaching for her hand, he pressed it between his palms. "Let's just say I've decided I want more than what I have now, Laurel. And I'm not talking about money."

"But wanting me—that doesn't make sense, Russ."

With a slight shake of his head, he bent and placed a kiss on her forehead. "It doesn't have to make sense," he murmured. "But I figure one of these days it will."

She opened her mouth to speak and for a split second Russ was tempted to kiss her again. But now was not the time to push things, he thought. There would be plenty of hours in the coming days to let Laurel know that he wanted her to be more than an assistant.

"Good night, Laurel," he said, then quickly walked out of the house before the desire to wrap her in his arms pushed away his common sense.

Laurel slept very little that night. In between fitful dozing, her mind was racing around in all different directions. Russ wanted her? Her! The idea was ridiculous. Even though he wasn't a sociable man, he was considered a very eligible bachelor in Lincoln County.

He had looks and wealth and had just now acquired a prestigious position with a prominent New Mexican ranch. He could have most any woman he set his sights on. One who was beautiful and elegant, one he could be proud to have on his arm and present to his friends and family.

Laurel wasn't blind. Whenever she looked in the mirror, she knew she was looking at an average woman with no special outward qualities. And as for the insides, she didn't want anyone, especially Russ, to see the many scars she was carrying. So why would he want her?

When the alarm went off at five, she stumbled out of bed in a groggy, exhausted state. While she quickly made coffee, she wondered how she'd be able to handle a day of work, much less face Russ again. On top of that, today was the last day the clinic would technically still be Hollister Animal Clinic, and that was enough to send her into tearful sobs.

She'd poured herself a cup of coffee and was about to spread jam on a piece of toast when she heard her cell phone alert for an incoming message.

Ignoring her simple breakfast, she picked up the phone and was surprised to see a short note from Russ.

Take the day off and finish unpacking. Maccoy and I will wind everything up at the clinic. R.

Feeling a bit deflated, she carried her meal to the kitchen table. While she sipped the coffee and munched the toast, she told herself it was probably better that she wasn't going to be at the clinic on this final day. It would be easier to bid farewell like this, away from the man who'd made everything about the place special.

Closing her gritty eyes, she pulled in a deep breath

and purposely straightened her shoulders. She'd coped with all sorts of disappointments and trials. She could deal with anything Russ threw at her, she promised herself. Including his bone-melting kisses.

Later that morning, Laurel managed to push aside Russ's behavior from the night before, and she got busy unpacking her belongings and storing them away in the many shelves and cabinets she'd discovered throughout the house. By late afternoon, the moving boxes were empty and most everything was in its place, so she decided to take a much-needed break and drive down to the main ranch house.

Since Laurel was familiar with the house, she went straight to the back and through the atrium, where a second door led into the kitchen.

After a quick knock, she stepped inside to find Reena Crowe, the family's longtime cook, standing at a worktable, chopping vegetables.

"May I come in?" she called as she stepped farther into the warm kitchen.

The cook looked up in surprise. "Laurel! How very nice to see you."

At the end of her fifties, Reena was still a lovely woman. Petite and slender, she had long salt-and-pepper hair that she braided and wound at the back of her head in an elegant chignon. Her slanted eyes were pale gray— even lighter than Laurel's gray eyes—and though the woman's Apache heritage was clearly evident, Laurel had to wonder if some of her family tree was mixed with white blood.

Smiling, Laurel said, "I brought your containers back. Thank you for the delicious meal. It was so thoughtful of you to send it to us." She placed the sack full of clean containers on the opposite end of the work-table, then reached to give the cook an affectionate hug. "It's wonderful to see you again. You look beautiful."

The other woman blushed and chuckled, "I'm past the beautiful stage, Laurel."

"Not you," Laurel argued. "And you haven't changed a bit since I was last here. And that's been a long time."

"Not since Alexa gave birth to her first little one, and that was three years ago," Reena agreed. She motioned for Laurel to sit on one of the high wooden stools near the worktable. "Have a seat. Would you like something to drink? I just made fresh coffee."

"That would be great. But let me get it. I know where everything is," Laurel insisted. "Don't let me interrupt your work. Would you like a cup, too?"

"Please. With cream and sugar," Reena told her.

After Laurel fixed the coffee and carried it back to the table, the two women took seats on the work stools.

"Mmm. I needed this," Laurel told her after she'd taken a long sip of the rich brew. "I've been unpacking all day."

Reena nodded. "So how do you like your house?"

Laurel didn't have to force a smile to her face—it came automatically. "It's great! I never expected the ranch to supply me with anything so spacious or nice. I'm going to love it." She glanced thoughtfully at the other woman. "Reena, didn't your mother live in that house, or am I confused about that?"

Nodding again, Reena said, "Yes. And I lived there with her until she passed away. The Cantrells had it built just for us. That's how generous they are—and always have been."

Laurel looked at her with dismay. "Oh, Reena, please

don't tell me you moved out so that I could have a place to stay! I wouldn't hear of it."

Laughing softly, Reena waved a dismissive hand at her. "Don't get worried. I haven't lived there since Momma died. It was just too hard. I saw her everywhere I looked. You understand?"

Only too well, Laurel thought. Once her sister had died, her father, Nels, and brother, Garth, had been tormented by the sight of Lainey's room, which Laurel had shared. Nels had immediately started talking about selling the place and moving on. But, thankfully, by the time a buyer had come along, Laurel was nearing the end of her senior year in high school. After that, both men had moved four hundred miles away to Arizona, running from the memories or their mistakes—Laurel wasn't sure which.

"Sure. I understand. So do you live here on the ranch now?"

"I have a small suite of rooms on the east end of the house. I'm very comfortable there. And with Alex and Quint living elsewhere now and Frankie away in Texas most of the time, no one lives here in the house except Laramie, the foreman of the ranch. And he's a single man."

Although Reena had a daughter, Laurel had never met the woman. From what Alexa had told her, Magena had moved away from the family many years ago. Laurel didn't know the whole story, but there had been some sort of rift over a man in Magena's life. And as far as Laurel knew, the break had never been repaired between mother and daughter. It was a sad situation, but then Laurel knew all too well about having a splintered family. Sometimes it was impossible to mend them back together.

Keeping her thoughts about Magena to herself, Laurel said, "I've not met the foreman yet, but I expect I will soon. Russ and I are going to look over our new work area tomorrow. I hear that Quint has spared no expense to create a small animal hospital for us."

"Quint has money to burn. And he wants every animal on the place to have the best of care. Plus he's smart enough to know that having Dr. Hollister here will help Laramie keep things running smoothly." She slowly sipped her coffee, then glanced thoughtfully at Laurel. "Do you think you'll like living here instead of town?"

Smiling wryly, Laurel shrugged. "It's going to be different. But it's beautiful out here and quiet. I'm going to enjoy that. And I'll get to ride horses—that's something I'll love."

The woman appeared pleased by her answer. "I'm glad, Laurel. I'm glad that you have found a home here. We all need that."

A home. Even before Lainey's illness, the Stantons had been far from a picture-perfect family. Her parents had often quarreled, mostly over bills and money. Her older brother had dropped out of high school and drifted from one paltry job to another. Even so, they'd all lived together in the same house and it had been home to Laurel.

But Lainey's disease caused something to click inside her mother, Stacie. The harried woman had fallen apart and, telling them all that she couldn't deal with the responsibility anymore, she'd packed a suitcase and left. After that, her father had gone into an indifferent sort of stupor, and Garth hadn't handled the situation any better. Both men had buried their heads in the sand and pretended that nothing was really the matter with anything or anyone, and had left all Lainey's care up to

Laurel. And once Lainey died, Nels and Garth had kept their distance from Laurel, as though they'd expected that she, too, would develop the illness, forcing them to care for her. It had been a great relief to her when she'd eventually grown old enough to strike out on her own. And she'd been that way ever since—alone and determined to be a better person than the relatives she'd once believed loved her.

"Yes, we all need a home," Laurel said softly.

Over the rim of her coffee cup, Reena studied her thoughtfully. "I've not yet met Dr. Hollister. He must be a very nice man and good at his job. Quint wouldn't hire a man without those qualities."

The mention of Russ caused warm color to spread across Laurel's face, forcing her to look away from the cook's perceptive gaze. "Russ is an excellent vet. And he's a very good man, too. Very fair and conscientious."

"You must enjoy working for him. Alexa tells me that you've been at his clinic for a long time."

Laurel nodded, while wondering what else her friend had told the cook about her relationship with Russ.

Why wonder about that, Laurel? You don't have a relationship with Russ. And at the rate you've been pushing him away, you aren't going to have one.

She turned her gaze back to Reena. "For five years. But today is the last day for the clinic. A new owner is taking over on Monday."

Reena's gentle smile was filled with compassion, as though she understood, without even being told, that Laurel was feeling a little torn about all the changes taking place.

"When an old door closes, you have to believe that a new and better one will open," Reena said gently. "You shouldn't worry, honey. The Chaparral will be a good place for you."

Laurel was beginning to think she must be walking around with the word *worry* written across her forehead. Everyone seemed to think she needed reassurance. If she was coming across as that weak and indecisive, then she needed to straighten her backbone. She might lack confidence in some aspects of her life, but not where her job was concerned. She'd made a commitment to work for the Chaparral, and she wasn't turning back for any reason. Even Russ.

"I feel so, too. Especially with you here." She leaned over far enough to wrap an affectionate arm around the cook's slender shoulders. "I've not had a mother in a long time. I hope you don't mind that I think of you in that way, Reena."

Patting Laurel's hand, she said in a husky voice, "It's been a long time since I've had a daughter, too. We'll be good for each other."

Early the next morning, Russ drove the short distance to Laurel's place. As he approached the house, he spotted her in the front yard playing with her two dogs, a gold shepherd mix and a black collie. With the sky completely clear, the sun was already bright. The light glinted off the patches of snow covering the ground and put a fiery glow on the loose hair flowing down her back.

Dressed in a pair of black jeans and a puffy red parka, she looked young and energetic as she taunted the dogs to race after her. It dawned on Russ that, even though he'd known Laurel for a long time, he'd never seen her outside work. Maybe that's why she looked so beautiful to him this morning. Why she'd looked so lovely and desirable Thursday night when the fire in the fireplace had started to burn. Along with his desire.

Spotting his arrival, she walked quickly through the gate to join him. His spirits suddenly soaring, Russ left the truck running and climbed to the ground to greet her.

"Good morning. Ready to go?"

"All set," she told him.

He glanced over her shoulder to where the dogs were still leaping and playing. "Aren't you going to put the dogs in the backyard?" he asked. "They can climb under this board fence."

"I've already turned them loose and let them run in the woods," she told him. "They know where their home is now. If they do leave, they won't go far. So I've let them have their freedom and they're loving it."

"No doubt," he agreed. The fact that she wasn't going to keep the pets locked behind a chain-link fence surprised him somewhat. Laurel had always been very protective when it came to her pets, almost overly so. But moving to the country could be changing her attitude, he thought.

He warned, "By nightfall their coats will be full of burrs and twigs."

"Yes, but they'll be happy dogs," she said with a shrug. "That's more important."

She started around to the passenger door of the truck, and Russ followed. As he opened the door and reached to give her an elbow up, she glanced around, her brows arched with question.

"Do I look sickly this morning or something?" she asked wryly.

"No. Actually you look quite fresh and beautiful," he said. "I just felt like being a gentleman this morning."

He could see that his remark had taken her aback somewhat, and with one boot resting on the running board, she paused to study his face.

"Then I suppose I'm expected to act like a lady."

He couldn't remember the last time he'd seen her hair loose like this, and before he could stop himself, he reached out and snared a few of the shiny chestnut tendrils between his fingers. "You *are* a lady, Laurel."

She didn't smile, but her eyes softened enough to tell him that she appreciated his words.

Suddenly clearing her throat, she said, "I think we'd better head on to the ranch yard."

His nearness was disturbing her, and though he wished she would move closer, just knowing that she wasn't indifferent to him had to be enough for right now. Over the past couple of days, he'd been fighting with himself, trying to tell himself that to win Laurel he would have to slow down and convince her he was serious. But this attraction he felt for his assistant had hit him suddenly, and the jolt had been so hard it was still reverberating through him. He didn't want to slow down. He wanted to grab her and show her what both of them had been missing.

"Yeah," he agreed. "Let's go."

He helped her into the cab and, after he'd joined her, he turned the truck away from her house. Across the console from him, she fastened her seat belt and settled back in the plush leather seat.

"How did things go at the clinic yesterday?" she asked. "Get everything wrapped up?"

"Yes. The last of the animals were picked up by their owners."

"Even Daisy, the German shepherd?" she wanted to know.

He smiled to himself. If there was one thing he truly knew about Laurel, she was totally devoted to the animals she treated. Nursing and nurturing were second nature to her. "Yes. Even Daisy. She's mending nicely, and her owners are going to bring her back to Dr. Brennan for follow-up treatments."

"So the new vet is moving in today," she mused aloud. "How does that make you feel?"

"Frankly, I feel good about it. Sometimes a person just knows when it's the right time to move on. And it was right for me." He glanced over to see her studying him closely. "What about you? Did you get everything unpacked yesterday?"

"Yes. Thank you for the day off. That was thoughtful of you."

He shot her a crooked grin. "I'm not an ogre all the time."

From the corner of his eye, he could see the palms of her hands moving up and down her thighs. She was nervous, and all he could think about was her and the way she'd made him feel when they'd kissed. Maybe she'd been right; maybe his overtures toward her had ruined their ability to work together. How was he going to be able to perform a delicate surgery with her standing next to him, reminding him how much he wanted to make love to her?

Russ wasn't going to think about the answer to that question. The fact that he was able to feel at all, to want a woman again, was too precious to resist or push away.

She said, "I've never thought of you as an ogre. A taskmaster, maybe, but not a monster."

A few yards ahead, the mountain lane connected to the primary dirt road that led to the main ranch house. Russ geared down the truck for the right turn.

"You don't have to tell me that I've pushed you at times, Laurel. But until we got away from the clinic, I guess I never realized just how hard I pushed," he said with a bit of regret. "If I ever hurt you because of it, I'm sorry."

The glance she shot him was so brief he didn't have the chance to read the expression on her face.

"Forget it," she murmured. "I'm sure there will be times you'll push me again. But there's no need for you to worry that you'll hurt me. I'm like an old piece of leather—too hard to tear."

And why would she ever think of herself as hard? Russ wondered. The Laurel he knew was soft inside and out. But he didn't know the whole Laurel, he reminded himself. He only knew the caring animal nurse who showed up to work beside him every day. He didn't know about her hopes and dreams or any of the things that made her the person that she was today.

When he'd married Brooke, he'd believed he'd known her completely. Now he looked back on his failed marriage and wondered if he'd been blind or simply a fool. Had he overlooked his ex-wife's flaws and weaknesses because he'd been so lonely and eager to start a family? Dear God, he couldn't make that mistake again, he told himself. He couldn't let himself be wrong about Laurel. He was drawn to her for many reasons, and this time he had to make sure those reasons were right.

"So you're tough, are you?" he asked with wry disbelief.

"As tough as I have to be."

Her voice was low, almost gritty, and Russ realized she was serious. Very serious.

Frowning, he glanced at her. "And what has turned

you into a piece of old leather? Or is that question too personal to ask?"

Shaking her head, she said, "I'm sorry, Russ. I didn't mean to sound so bitter. But, well, as a child I went through some things that would have torn the heart out of a strong adult."

After a moment, he guessed, "Your sister?"

Bending her head, she nodded. "Yes. I'll tell you all about it someday—when I'm able."

It was hard for Russ to imagine what losing her twin must have done to her, and though he wanted to know more about her personal life, he wasn't going to push her to relate it. She'd never pressed him for intimate details about himself; he had to do the same for her and respect her privacy. And hope that someday she would feel close enough to want to share those dark times and all the rest of it with him.

"And I'll listen," he said, "whenever you're able."

He felt her look at him and glanced over to see a faint smile curving her lips.

"I'll remember that, Russ."

Shadows darkened her gray eyes, yet there was a glint of gratefulness shining through to him, and the sight touched something deep in the middle of his chest.

It was often said that a man's treasure was hidden in plain sight. Russ was beginning to see that he'd found his, and he wasn't about to let himself lose sight of her.

Chapter Six

A few minutes later, the huge, two-story ranch house, with its walls of cedar and native rock, appeared on the far horizon.

As it did, Laurel spoke. "I drove down here to the big house yesterday—to return the food containers to Reena and thank her for the meal."

"That was thoughtful of you."

"I've known Reena for a long time," she explained. "Ever since Alexa and I became friends in elementary school. When we were teenagers she was almost like my mother."

All this time, when Russ had been making plans to accept the job post here on the Chaparral, he'd never guessed that Laurel had such deep ties to the place. Quint had mentioned, almost in passing, that Russ's assistant was an old friend of his sister's, but that had been the extent of their conversation on the matter. Now

Russ was getting the feeling that she'd spent lots of time in the Cantrell home.

"I didn't realize you were so familiar with folks here on the ranch."

She shrugged. "I'm ashamed to admit that I've let months go by without keeping in contact with Reena." She cast him a curious glance. "Did you know Lewis? Quint and Alexa's father?"

Russ nodded. "Yes. I used to see Lewis and Frankie at the racetrack in Ruidoso."

"That's surprising. I didn't know you ever took the time to visit the track," she said with faint disbelief.

"That was when I first started the clinic and didn't have the facilities built for horses to occupy, so I frequently took calls at the track," he explained, then shook his head at the recollection. "Damn, but that was a long time ago. Years, in fact."

"You've come a long way since then," she said. "And so many changes have occurred here on the Chaparral, too. Lewis died, and then Alexa and Quint learned that their mother had been married earlier in her life to a man in Texas, and that they had half brothers they'd never met."

"Yes, I remember," he said. "That got the gossip mills in town turning at full speed. But instead of tearing the family apart, the scandal seemed to pull them even tighter together. There are plenty of folks who could take lessons from the Cantrells," he said.

The Stantons certainly could have learned a lot from them, Laurel thought. But it was too late for her family now. As for Russ's, she knew hardly anything about his relatives. He'd mentioned his mother to her once and that had come unexpectedly, after he'd been forced to end a mare's suffering from being caught and stranded in barbed wire for several days.

The loss had hit him harder than usual, and as the two of them had been traveling back to the clinic, he'd brought up his mother and the fact that he'd lost her to cancer, and how helpless he'd felt because there was nothing he could do to save her. At the time, she'd remembered thinking how she'd felt the same way when Lainey had died, but she'd not shared those bleak memories with him. The two of them never talked about their families or private lives. Along with that, Laurel had never felt comfortable talking about her late twin, but on that occasion she'd been tempted to. Weeks later, it had dawned on Laurel that the day Russ had mentioned his mother had been Mother's Day, and the realization that he'd been remembering and grieving had brought a sting of tears to her eyes. It had also reminded her that he was more than a rock-hard man with a fanatical work ethic. He was human, fully capable of hurting. Just like her.

Shaking away the emotional memories, Laurel noticed they had reached the ranch-yard proper and Russ had steered the truck onto a roadway that ran between two enormous barns. At the end of the building on the left, he parked next to a white four-wheel-drive truck with The Chaparral and its brand printed on the driver's door. A few feet to the right stood the building and its large door with a window at the top. Above the window swung a shingle with the name Dr. Russ Hollister branded into the wood.

"I was here a couple of weeks ago to see how the construction work was progressing, but the workers still had everything in a mess," he told her. "Let's go see how things are looking now."

When the two of them stepped inside, Laurel was totally stunned. Even though Reena had told her that Quint was sparing no expense, she'd never expected him to supply Russ with such a modern and spacious office.

As she stepped farther into the room, she practically gasped. "Wow! This looks like Italian tile on the floor. And the furniture—it's so beautiful."

Scurrying over to a long couch, she ran a hand over the soft, wine-red leather. There were two matching armchairs flanking it, and across the room, facing each other, sat two separate cherrywood desks, each manned with a computer, telephone, Rolodex and other amenities needed to run a business. At the opposite end of the room, a countertop ran the length of one wall and behind the waist-high partition, Maccoy was busy placing manila files on built-in wooden shelves.

Laurel waved a greeting to the older man, then turned her attention to another part of the office, where a tall cowboy wearing a black hat and jingle-bell spurs was pouring himself a cup of coffee from an up-to-the-minute coffee machine.

As soon as the man spotted Laurel and Russ, he set the coffee aside and strode quickly over to greet them.

"I thought you'd be here soon," he said as he reached to shake Russ's hand.

The two men exchanged greetings and then Russ motioned to her. "Laramie, this is my assistant, Laurel Stanton. I hate to admit it," he said with a teasing grin, "but I can't work without her, so I was forced to bring her along."

"I'm sure you didn't have to have your arm twisted to hold on to her," the foreman said to Russ. Then, giving Laurel a quiet but charming smile, he reached to shake her hand.

"It was more like I had to twist hers," Russ admitted to the other man, then turned his gaze on Laurel. "This is Laramie Jones, and just in case you don't know, he's the foreman of the Chaparral. What he says, goes."

Laramie chuckled at Russ's remark. "Quint might argue with you there."

The ranch foreman was somewhere near thirty, Laurel guessed, and very attractive in a dark and rugged way. Yet meeting him wasn't making her heart skip a beat. No man did that to her, except Russ, she thought helplessly.

"It's very nice to meet you, Laramie," she told the foreman. "Alexa is always praising you, so you must be very good at your job."

The faint grin on his face deepened as he finally dropped her hand. "From the way Quint talks about you and Russ, I'm expecting you two to be able to walk on water."

Chuckling, Russ exchanged a pointed look with her. "He's in for a disappointment, isn't he?"

"I'm afraid so," Laurel joked along with the two men.

Laramie gestured toward the room surrounding them. "So what do you think about the office?" he asked. "Quint's made an endless number of trips out here to make sure the contractors would have it all finished in time."

"The last time I looked, the walls were still bare Sheetrock. I never expected it to turn out like this," Russ told him. "I'm not sure I'm going to know how to work in this luxury. My office in town was a dusty little cubbyhole with a metal desk, one file cabinet and a couple of folding chairs for my customers."

"And a closet we turned into a snack room. Don't forget to mention that," Laurel chimed in.

"Shhh, Laurel! You're making me sound cheap," Russ joked.

"Not cheap. Just practical," she corrected, then smiled at Laramie. "He spent all his extra money on his patients. Trust me."

Laramie smiled back at her. "A dedicated man. Glad to hear it." Turning his gaze back to Russ, he gestured to a door leading out of the office and into another part of the building. "Let's go look at the rest of your work area. And you can let me know if anything won't work or what else you might need."

She and Russ followed the ranch foreman through the door and into a huge room with a scrupulously clean concrete floor, two squeeze chutes for cattle, a pair of small pens to hold recovering animals, a horse-examining gate, a long row of cabinets lining one wall and two treatment tables, along with a huge double sink.

Fascinated by the up-to-date facilities, Laurel quickly strode over to the cabinets and began to inspect all the equipment hidden behind the metal doors. "Russ, come look at this! There's everything we need and more," she exclaimed.

He joined her at the work counter, and for the next few minutes the two of them were like kids in a toy store as they inspected the enormous amount of drugs and veterinary supplies stacked inside the cabinets.

"We've kept the drug cabinet locked. I only opened it this morning because I knew you were coming," Laramie told Russ. "Now that you're here, I'm handing the key over to you."

Russ thanked him and pocketed the pair of ringed keys. "Do you think it'll be necessary for me to keep it locked?" Russ asked him. "I don't want the ranch hands to think I consider them thieves. And there will be times that I'm not here that you'll need certain medications."

Laramie shook his head. "We have a great group of honest men here, Russ. They understand that you can't leave narcotics sitting about. Otherwise, we'll figure out what to do if an emergency arises and you're not here."

"Don't worry," Laurel couldn't help but add, "Russ will always be here. He doesn't do anything else but work."

The foreman exchanged an amused look with Russ. "She sounds like she knows you."

Russ grunted. "She only *thinks* she knows me."

He was right about that, Laurel thought, as she followed the two men into a sparkling operating room. After five years of working with the man, Laurel had believed that she knew Russ. But in the past couple of weeks, he'd taken her by complete surprise. Not only had he shocked her with this move to the Chaparral, he'd stunned her with his kisses and the insinuation that he wanted to have some sort of relationship with her.

A few minutes later, Laramie left them on their own, and as she joined Russ on another leisurely tour through the work area, the last pangs of lingering nostalgia she was carrying for the old clinic dissolved at the eager and pleased expression on Russ's face.

When an old door closes, you have to believe that a new and better one will open. Reena's words seemed especially fitting, Laurel thought. Russ had worked so hard for so many years. He deserved this special clinic and all the benefits that went with it.

As he stood looking over one of the treatment tables, Laurel felt compelled to move closer, and once she was at his side, she laid a hand on his arm. The contact drew his gaze to hers and she gave him a small smile.

"I'm very happy for you, Russ. You deserve all of this."

The soft light in his eyes said her words had touched him, and the notion filled her with a strange sort of joy.

"I'm not so sure I deserve it," he told her. "But thanks for the thought."

With a gentle shake of her head, she said, "Yes. You do deserve it. Because now that you've made a commitment, I know that you'll give this ranch all of yourself. Just like you did with the clinic in town."

Something flickered in his eyes before he turned to fully face her. "Not all of me, Laurel," he corrected, his voice suddenly going low and husky. "Part of me needs more than work. Part of me needs you."

She drew in a sharp breath, and though the tone of his voice warned her to step back and away from him, she was too mesmerized to do anything but stare up at him.

"Russ— I—" She nervously licked her lips and started again. "Didn't you hear a word I said the other night?"

One corner of his lips curved upward. "Didn't you hear anything I said?"

She swallowed. "I was serious."

"So was I," he murmured.

Groaning, she said, "You clearly have your wants and your needs mixed up, Russ."

Shaking his head, he stepped forward and slid both arms around her waist until his hands were linked at the small of her back and his forehead pressed against hers. Laurel had never felt her heart beat so hard or fast.

"I've been telling myself that I need to give you time to let you think about all of this—about me. But when we're together, I can see that sort of thinking is stupid. Neither of us are kids. Nor are we strangers."

"And those are sensible excuses for us to fall into each other's arms?"

His chuckle was low and sinfully sexy. "Why do we need excuses? Why isn't wanting each other enough?"

Maybe if she was a normal woman, it would be, she thought, as a sense of helpless desire began to course through her veins. Maybe then she wouldn't worry about making love to this man or what it might do to her mangled heart.

"I don't know." Her throat was so tight her voice came out as little more than a whisper, and before she could stop herself, her eyes closed and his name whispered past her lips.

"Oh, Laurel, I'm so sorry," he murmured as his fingertips traced a featherlight path across her cheek. "Sorry I've been blind for so long. But I wasn't looking or even thinking." His head bent until his lips were poised over hers. "I wasn't even feeling, Laurel. But I am now. And I don't plan to stop."

Laurel wasn't sure if she closed the last bit of distance between their lips or if Russ did. Either way, it didn't matter. All that mattered was the warm magic his lips were creating upon hers, the gentle eagerness of his hands roaming against her back, drawing her closer.

She must have been crazy, she thought, for believing there was ever a chance of her resisting this man. Touching him, loving him, felt as natural and good as drawing in a deep, sweet breath on a warm spring morning.

Mindlessly, her arms lifted and curled around his neck, her body arched into his. Her senses were like a slow, hot whirlpool, swirling around and around until she forgot they were in a workplace where anyone could walk in on them.

But both of them were suddenly reminded of their

whereabouts when the sound of an outer door opening and closing registered in Laurel's fuzzy brain.

She spun out of his arms so quickly that she stumbled, and if not for his steadying hold on her arm, she would have fallen to the concrete floor.

"That was in another part of the building," he quickly reassured her.

His voice was low and husky as he tugged her back around to him, and Laurel was shocked at how much she wanted to step back into the circle of his arms and let her body melt against his.

Shoving her tumbled hair back from her face, she finally managed to speak. "Thank goodness someone reminded us we're supposed to be working."

"We're not starting work until Monday," he reminded her. "But maybe we'd better take this up later—in a more private place."

If she had any backbone at all she would tell him there wasn't going to be any "later" and that the kiss they'd just shared was going to be their last. But her senses were still a shaky, vulnerable mess from her being in his arms. Right now she wasn't in any condition to put up a convincing argument, much less persuade herself that she could resist him.

Turning away from him, she started out of the treatment area. "I'm going back out front and see if Maccoy wants to have a cup of coffee with me," she told him.

"Am I invited, too?"

He was following close on her heels and she didn't bother to glance over her shoulder at him as she answered, "You're the boss. You're going to do what you want, anyway."

"Not when it comes to you, Laurel."

That brought her up short and she quickly spun around to face him. "What does that mean?"

His expression went soft and serious. "It means I won't ever take anything from you unless you want to give it to me. Any other way just wouldn't be good for me. Understand?"

Suddenly her throat was too thick to speak, so she nodded, then turned and continued out of the room.

Laurel spent the remainder of the morning helping Maccoy arrange files, while Russ toured the foaling and calving barns. Later, Laramie invited her and Russ on a tour to see some of the outer working areas of the ranch. With most of the landscape remote and rough, they were forced to travel in an older, dual-wheeled truck with a single cab and one bench seat.

Each time the vehicle hit a bump or hole, Laurel's thigh and shoulder would rub against Russ's, making it almost impossible to keep her mind on the reason they were driving through the wilderness in the first place. She'd never been so aware of a man in her life, so attuned to his masculine scent, the heat of his body, the timbre of his voice. He'd said he'd been blind during these past years they'd worked together, and Laurel had thought that explanation was feeble at best. After all, there hadn't been a day go by without her taking note of his handsome face and rugged sexuality. But today, after they'd kissed so passionately, she'd realized that she'd not exactly been seeing all of him, either. There were so many things about him that she'd never noticed before, so many sides of him she knew nothing about. But desperately wanted to.

By the time they headed home, darkness had already arrived to the dense forest surrounding Laurel's house.

As he parked the truck in front of the yard gate, he said, "We made a much longer day of it than I'd planned. Are you tired?"

"A bit," she conceded, "but today was a breeze compared to a day at the clinic." She unbuckled her seat belt and slipped on her coat. "Would you like to come in for a while? I'll make coffee and sandwiches."

His brows shot up. "Are you serious?"

He was clearly surprised by the invitation and Laurel could understand why. Each time he'd taken one step toward her, she'd been taking one step back. But somewhere between that kiss this morning and the drive home this evening, something had happened to her. She'd kept thinking about all the years she'd worked with Russ and all those secret dreams and feelings for him that she'd carried around and clung to like a child to her favorite blanket.

For years, a part of her had longed for him to look at her in a romantic way, while the other part had felt safe in the fact that he never would. Now that he had, her first instinct had been to run far and fast. But she was so very tired of running. If only for a little while, she wanted to feel like a woman. She wanted to live out her cherished dreams.

"Yes, I'm serious. But if you'd rather get on home, that's okay, too."

He turned off the truck engine and reached for his coat. "I'd love to eat with you," he told her.

As soon as they exited the truck, the dogs were there to greet them and Laurel laughed as she spotted the mud and twigs matted in their coats.

"Well, you warned me," she told Russ, then patted both dogs on the head. "But you're a pair of happy guys, aren't you?"

For answer, the canines barked and ran in excited circles around Laurel and Russ as they made their way to the front entrance of the house.

"I didn't lock the door," she told him as she reached around the door jamb and flipped on a light in the tiny foyer. "But if I'd known we were going to be out this late, I would have left the porch light on."

"I didn't lock my house, either. But Leo's there. He'd scare anything away," Russ joked as he followed her into the house.

A few minutes later, after they'd both visited the bathroom to freshen up, Laurel got busy in the kitchen putting a small meal together, while Russ built a fire in the fireplace.

The wood was already burning nicely when Laurel appeared in the living room carrying the sandwiches and coffee on a wooden tray.

"I have to confess I tried building a fire yesterday, but it just wouldn't burn for me," she told him as she bent to place the tray on the coffee table.

"Why don't you bring that over here?" he suggested. "We can eat here on the rug in front of the fire."

Two nights ago, sitting in front of the fire had gotten her into more trouble than she'd known how to handle, but she wasn't going to let that scare her away tonight. She needed to show him and herself that she was a mature woman and unafraid.

"All right," she agreed. "It's getting so cold outside the extra heat would feel nice."

Laurel settled the tray between them, and while they ate the turkey-and-cheese sandwiches, they discussed everything they'd witnessed out on the range with Laramie.

"You know," Laurel said thoughtfully, "I've been

friends of the Cantrells for years and visited the ranch on many occasions. I knew it was a huge ranch, but after seeing parts of it today, I realize it's more than huge—it's massive."

Having finished the last of her sandwich, she put the plate back on the tray and poured more coffee into her mug.

He said, "That surprises me. I figured Alexa and Quint had shown you all around the place before."

She watched him set his empty plate next to hers, then stretching out on his side, he propped up his head with one hand. The relaxed position spelled lazy sexuality, and try as she might, she couldn't make her gaze look at anything else but him.

Ignoring the strange pitter-patter of her pulse, she said, "At times Alexa and I went horseback riding, but we never ventured too far away from the house. Some of the areas Laramie drove us over today were so remote I was beginning to think we might end up having to walk back to the ranch yard."

"So what did you think about the foreman?" he asked.

She reached for her coffee. "He's a man of few words."

"He's part Comanche. It's his nature to listen rather than talk."

Her brows peaked with interest. "How would you know that? You know some Comanches personally?"

He surprised her by nodding. "When I went to college. I became friends with one and got acquainted with his family. They're horse people. It goes way back in their ancestry. Nocona, that was my buddy's name, was studying to be a vet specializing in horse care."

"Hmm. Guess that's why Laramie seems to know

horses inside out. Cattle, too, for that matter. And that's going to make your job lots easier."

A slight smile curved his lips. "That's true, but before you start thinking it's going to be a breeze for us around here, I'd better warn you there will be times, like calving and foaling season, when you and I will get very little sleep. And I look for all of that to start up any day now."

Her gaze continued to wander over the long length of his body until it finally settled on the rugged lines of his face. She figured at one time in his very young years his hair had been more golden-blond. Now it was closer to light brown with gold-and-amber streaks threaded through the parts that were exposed to the sun. Faint lines fanned from the corners of his eyes and bracketed his lips, while his day-old whiskers partially hid the faint dent in his chin. Over these past five years, she'd studied his face many times. The way each feature complemented the next. The way the colors of his skin and hair and eyes came together to form a rich, gold-brown hue. But she'd never been able to really read his expressions that well.

She said, "Hard work has never scared me, Russ. You should know that by now."

His brown eyes met hers. "No. Work never scared you," he agreed. "But I sure as hell do."

She stared at him as her pulse leaped to an even faster pace. "What does that mean? I've never been afraid to stand up to you. After all, the most you can do is fire me. And being fired doesn't kill a person."

He grimaced. "Hell, as far as work goes, you stand up to me because you and I both know I'd never fire you. No, your fear has to do with something altogether different."

"You're wrong," she said flatly.

The only thing separating the two of them was the tray of leftovers, and Laurel defenselessly watched him push it aside to clear the space between them.

"Am I?" He moved closer until his hand was wrapped around her upper arm and his face was hovering closer to hers. "I don't think so. This scares you, Laurel. Having me touch you, kiss you."

Emotions were suddenly blocking her throat, forcing her to swallow. "Why would you think that? I told you that it was nice. Just because I'm inexperienced doesn't mean I'm afraid."

His hand came up to her face, and Laurel felt her bones turn to hot liquid as his rough palm cupped the side of her cheek. "But you are," he countered, his voice low and seductive. "You kiss me, all right, but I can feel a part of you trembling and ready to bolt at any moment. Why, Laurel?"

How could she answer his question when she couldn't even explain it to herself? she wondered helplessly.

"Okay, so I am a little scared," she admitted in a choked voice. "But this is— It's all new to me. And it's not anything I planned on."

His head pulled back far enough for him to look into her eyes. "You can't plan attraction or love, Laurel. It just happens. Haven't you learned that by now?"

Closing her eyes, a sigh slipped past her lips. "How could I? I've never been in love. I've never really wanted anyone until you."

He groaned. "Oh, Laurel. Laurel. Don't be afraid of me. Of this. I could never hurt you. Ever."

Suddenly he pulled her down beside him on the warm rug, and as his lips found hers and his kiss swept her up in a torrent of hot desire, she realized she didn't want to think about being afraid or running for dear life. She wanted to hang on to him with every fiber of her being. She wanted to find out for herself what it really meant for a woman to surrender herself to love.

Chapter Seven

Laurel had lost her mind. Why else would she have tempted fate and recklessly invited Russ to join her for sandwiches and coffee when she'd known—the both of them had known—what would happen.

Because she was tired of fighting her feelings, tired of running and hiding from the very thing she'd wanted for so long, she silently answered the questioning voice in her head.

She might be crazy, and tomorrow she'd probably find herself sick with regret, but for tonight she was going to bravely reach for all the joy this man could give her.

And like a tumbleweed gathered up by a fierce wind, Laurel felt herself being totally swept away by the hungry search of his lips upon hers, the hot urgency of his hands as they roamed over her back, down to her buttocks and back up to her breasts, where his fingers kneaded the soft flesh.

Behind them, the flames in the fireplace were throwing out waves of heat, but it couldn't begin to compare to the sizzle rushing through Laurel as his tongue plunged past her teeth and invited her tongue to mate with his. The intimate connection filled Laurel with uncontrollable heat and summoned a moan deep within her throat.

Just as she was becoming lost to the erotic things he was doing to her mouth, his hands returned to her hips and tugged the lower half of her body tightly against his. Laurel didn't need experience to understand the language of his body. She was reading it loud and clear. Yet she was helpless to turn away or deny either of them.

When he finally tore his mouth from hers, he sucked in a fierce breath then whispered against her ear. "Do you know what you're doing, Laurel? I want to make love to you. If that's not what you want, then I've got to stop and get the hell out of here. Understand?"

With his thumbs resting against her cheeks and his hands bracketing her face, he tilted her face so that their gazes could meet. And as Laurel looked at him, she could do little more than nod.

"Yes. I understand," she finally managed to say.

One hand eased away from her face and came up to gently stroke a tangle of reddish-brown hair off her forehead.

"And?"

"And I don't want you to leave."

The moment the solemn answer passed her lips, a look of triumph flickered in his eyes and without another word, he rose from the rug and pulled her along with him.

As he led her out of the room and across the short

hallway to her bedroom, Laurel felt like a sleeping princess in a dream. Everything around her seemed too hazy to be real. Even the darkness of the bedroom held a velvety softness that enveloped the two of them like a warm cloak. But if she was sleeping, she could only hope his kisses didn't wake her.

A few short steps inside the bedroom, Laurel left his side long enough to switch on a small lamp near the head of the bed. For a brief moment the golden-hued circle of light penetrated the foggy haze of her desire and a voice inside her head began to scream at her to run, to save herself from the heartache that was sure to follow these forbidden moments with Russ.

But before she could let the doubtful voice sway her, Russ was at her side, drawing her back into the tight circle of his arms.

"I feel goose bumps," he murmured as his hands dipped beneath her sweater and eased around to her back. "If you're cold, I'd better do something about it."

Her laugh came out sounding more like a choked cry. "It's cooler in here. But I'm not cold. Not with your arms around me."

He must have liked her answer, because he dropped another kiss on her lips before he guided her over to the edge of the mattress. As she stood on the tip of her toes, seeking the pleasure of his mouth once again, the last lingering bits of Laurel's shyness evaporated.

Her fingers quickly began to fumble with the buttons on his shirt. Once they were released and the fabric fell open, it set off a chain reaction that had him rapidly shrugging out of the garment, then shedding the black thermal top he was wearing beneath. Once it was out of the way and his torso was bare, he turned to her.

In a matter of seconds he pulled her sweater over her

head, then unhooked her bra and slid it off her arms. The moment her breasts were exposed to his sight, he paused to curve his hands around their fullness, then slowly, purposely, his head bent to place a kiss on each budded pink nipple.

The sensation of his lips touching her heated skin sent her senses spinning. With a shocked gasp, her head fell limply backward and she clutched the sides of his waist in order to keep her balance.

"Oh, Russ... I think the floor must be tilting or I'm very, very drunk."

Chuckling, he eased her back onto the mattress. "That's the way you're supposed to feel, my darling."

The endearment melted her, and with her eyes half closed and her heart beating wildly, she watched him remove her jeans and boots, then quickly deal with the remainder of his clothing.

His strong, stocky build had always appealed to her, but the moment it was truly exposed to her, she very nearly lost her breath. His broad shoulders and arms were wide and thick with muscle, his waist lean and hard. Curly brown hair grew between his flat nipples, then downward in a V shape that ended at his navel. Below his waist, his long legs and thighs were a picture of power.

Yet it was the sight of his manhood, erect with desire, that thoroughly jolted her. She'd seen pictures of naked men before, but she'd never seen one in the flesh, and to say that Russ was all man would have been an understatement.

She needed to tell him that she'd never been with a man before, she quickly told herself. He needed to know that he would be her first and that she'd never wanted to have sex with a man until she'd met him.

But she was thirty years old. He'd probably think she was lying. And even if he did believe her, the whole thing was too embarrassing. It might even give him the idea that she was in love with him, and she wasn't. She couldn't be!

Before she could decide what to do or how to explain anything to him, he was already lying next to her and rolling her body close to his. Sensations suddenly swamped her as his leg slung possessively over hers, and the hair on his chest brushed against her puckered nipples.

"I've imagined how you might look naked in my arms and I thought it would be good," he said lowly as one hand wandered over the curve of her waist and slipped onto her hip. "But I never dreamed you'd look this good. Or right."

He'd dreamed of having her in his arms? The idea stung her eyes with tears, and she wrapped her arms around him and pressed her cheek to the middle of his chest. "Russ, I'm a plain woman," she said with a rush of emotion. "I don't understand what you're seeing, but you make me feel special anyway. Very special."

With his thumb and forefinger wrapped around her chin, he tilted her face away from his chest in order to look at her. "Oh, Laurel, that's because you are special." His fingers moved away from her chin to trace the outline of her puffy lips. "You don't need paint on your face to make you beautiful. Your lips are naturally pink and so are your cheeks. Your eyes are the color of a gray dove. But what makes them even prettier is their softness. I've never seen you look at anything or anyone with anger or hate, and that's what makes them truly beautiful."

The tears stinging her eyes suddenly pooled and silently slipped onto her cheeks. "Russ, I— There's something you ought to know before—"

Her words paused as he wiped away the trickles of moisture with his forefinger. "There's no need for you to explain anything, Laurel. I understand this thing between us is happening quickly and I know you have reservations about it, but I don't want you to fret about those now—or ever. The years we've been together have been good. And they're going to keep on being good."

She responded with an anguished murmur. "That's not what I need to talk to you about tonight. This is something— Oh, God, this is so embarrassing—"

Her voice trailed away. But rather than pressure her to finish, his expression turned tender and he bent his head to press a cheek against hers. "My sweet Laurel. If you're worried about birth control, I can deal with that problem."

"I'm not worried about birth control. I'm on the Pill. Not for sexual reasons," she added quickly, her face flaming with heat. "To keep my cycle regulated."

He eased his head back far enough to look at her, and some of the angst she'd been feeling vanished at the understanding smile on his face. "I'm a doctor, Laurel. I know all about those sorts of things. You can't tell me anything about your body that could possibly shock me."

Seeing there was no easy way, she suddenly blurted, "Even if I told you I was a virgin?"

The fingers caressing her hip halted as he stared at her. "A virgin?"

Just having the word out in the open gave her a measure of relief and the confidence to reach for him.

With her hands making a gentle foray of his broad chest and down to his rock-hard waist, she answered,

"You said you couldn't be shocked, but you are. I can see it on your face."

His head swung back and forth in disbelief. "I did tell you that, but I wasn't expecting you to tell me something like this! Something that's hard to believe. You're—"

She grimaced. "Thirty years old," she finished for him. "I guess that makes me sound like a freak or an old maid or whatever you want to label me."

Easing up on one elbow, he frowned at her. "I don't want to label you, Laurel! I want to make love to you. But now—"

Russ's voice trailed away as all sorts of thoughts raced through his head. If he had one ounce of decency in him, he'd pull on his clothes and get the hell out of here. But as he gazed down at Laurel's lovely face, he couldn't ignore how much he wanted her. Probably more than he'd ever wanted any woman in his life.

Drawing in a long, cleansing breath, he tried to wrap his mind around the fact that she was still an innocent, that she'd never given herself to a man. What did it mean that she'd chosen him to be the one?

With another shake of his head, he said, "I don't understand why you've waited so long, Laurel. Why—"

"Have I never had sex before?" She completed the question for him.

She turned her face away from his as though she wanted to hide from him, or her past, or both.

"Okay," she said with a sigh, "if you really must know, I never met anyone I wanted to be that close to." She glanced back at him, a mocking twist on her lips. "Oh, there were a few guys in high school and college who tried to get me into their beds, but I wasn't interested in their games."

The flat emptiness in her voice bothered Russ greatly.

He didn't want to think she'd been hurt and disillusioned by any man. "Is that what you thought—that it was all just games? You never considered that one of them might have been in love with you? Or that you loved him?"

"No. I'm not sure I know what being in love is all about."

Her response only filled him with more questions. It was clear that something or someone had shaped her life and steered it away from finding intimacy.

But she was seeking it tonight—with him. For now that had to be enough to satisfy his doubts.

"Well, that hardly makes you unique. I'm not sure anyone knows exactly what being in love is all about."

Her gaze suddenly dropped from his and her lips began to tremble. Russ desperately wanted to kiss away her doubts and pains, he wanted to show her, reassure her, that she wasn't abnormal—she was a beautiful, desirable woman.

Cradling her face between his hands, he asked, "Laurel, haven't you ever dreamed about loving a man? Marrying him and having his children?"

Her dark lashes drifted down, but not before he saw tormented shadows turn her gray eyes to cold slate.

"Yes, I've dreamed," she whispered. "But dreams are different from the real thing."

She opened her eyes, and the look he saw in their depths was suddenly desperate and pleading. "Let's not talk about this tonight, Russ. I'm here in your arms because I want to be. Isn't that enough?"

It wasn't, Russ realized. Not really. Her evasiveness bothered him and he wanted to think there was more to their going to bed together than just sex. He wanted to think that he mattered to her, in all the ways a man could matter to a woman. But to press the issue would make it sound as though he was asking for her love. And he could see she was hardly ready for anything that serious. But would she ever be?

He couldn't let himself think or worry about that question tonight. She was already offering him more than he'd ever expected. He had to take it, run with it and hope that love would come later.

Bending his head, he brushed his lips over her cheeks and nose and finally her lips. "Yes, my sweet, it's enough," he murmured. "But I want you to be sure. You've waited this long. Maybe I'm not the right man and then you'll hate me for taking your innocence."

All of a sudden, her arms wrapped around his neck and she pulled him tight against her. "You are the right man, Russ. The *only* man I want in my bed."

His failed marriage had left his ego battered and he'd come away from it feeling worse than unwanted. Now Laurel was saying *he* was the only man she wanted. The words were like a soothing balm to his wounded heart.

"Laurel. Laurel. I don't know why you chose me. But I'm damned glad you did."

He found her lips, and as she kissed him sweetly, fervently, he didn't have to wonder why he was here in her bed. She molded perfectly to his body and matched his life even better. She had to know that. Had to feel it each time he touched her.

For the next few minutes, Russ forced himself to keep things slow and gentle, even though it was taking a supreme effort to keep the heat inside him from exploding.

Over and over he kissed her lips until the need to taste more than her mouth finally demanded that he turn his attention elsewhere. As his lips skimmed along the length of her throat, he thought how she tasted sweet and rich, like butter-smooth candy. One bite and he wanted more. So much more.

Her rounded breasts were full, the small rosy nipples taut with desire. His tongue laved each of them until she was moaning and arching upward to bring her breasts even closer to his mouth. Her fingers dug into his hair and clamped against his scalp as though she wanted to hold him there forever. The eager reaction heated his blood to the boiling point, until every cell in his body felt ready to explode.

Forced to lift his head and catch his breath, he whispered in a raw, husky voice, "I don't want to hurt you, Laurel. But I can't wait much longer."

"You don't have to wait." The corners of her lips tilted invitingly upward as she pulled his upper body back down to hers. "I'm ready, Russ. More than ready for you to make me a woman."

He'd planned to use his fingers first, to stroke and prime her for the shock that was to follow. But desire had him in a mindless grip and he could feel his self-control rapidly slipping away. He had no choice now but to couple their bodies and find the release they both desperately needed.

Parting her legs, he slowly, gently began to enter the dark, velvety depths of her, and just when he thought he couldn't bear to draw out the pace any longer, she clamped her hands on his buttocks and thrust her hips up to his.

The movement ended his agony with breathtaking pleasure, but as his ears caught the fierce intake of her breath, he realized it was probably the complete opposite for her. Most likely she felt as though he was going to split her apart.

Bending his head, he quickly brought his lips down

to hers. "Laurel, I'm sorry! I don't want to hurt you. But I can't stop! I can't!"

"Oh, Russ. It's okay. Really okay," she whispered against his cheek. "Just make love to me."

Along with her words, he could feel her body settling around his, her arms and legs circling him, her mouth planting rapid-fire kisses along his neck and on his shoulder. Her eager response was all that was needed to spur his hips into a thrusting rhythm. Laurel immediately began to match his pace, and in that instant his ability to think dissolved in a violent whirl of passion.

After that, time spun wildly out of control, making it impossible for Russ to know how much of it had passed before his body was drenched with sweat and his lungs burned for air. But the ticking minutes held no consequence for him. All that mattered was Laurel's soft body writhing beneath him, her hands skimming over his skin, her lips feeding hungrily on his mouth, and the moans in her throat growing into deep, needy growls.

He couldn't let it end, he thought. He couldn't let the ecstasy slip away. But his body refused to listen to his brain, and before he could slow their momentum, he could feel the two of them blending as one, racing faster and faster, until his breaths were nothing but harsh rasps and blood pounded in his ears, blocking out every sound, every thought but her and all that she was giving him.

The end was like tumbling down a steep mountain and hitting the ravine below with a sharp jolt. The landing was so stunning it took several moments for him to gather his whereabouts and finally realize he was lying atop Laurel, his face buried in the curve of her shoulder.

Quickly, he eased his weight off her, but kept his

hand firmly attached to her waist as he settled himself close to her side.

"Please tell me you're okay."

His voice sounded choked and unrecognizable to his own ears. Had making love to her already changed him that much?

Slowly, she turned and curved her arm possessively across his chest. "Mmm. I'm fine."

He reached to touch her hair and discovered his hand was trembling. The realization stunned him. He was a big, strong man who stayed in shape. A soft little woman like her shouldn't have the power to make him this weak and vulnerable, he thought. But she had. In more ways than one.

"I'm glad. I couldn't have forgiven myself if your first time ended up being a nightmare."

Turning her face slightly, she pressed a kiss to his shoulder. "It was special, Russ. So special."

How could one word make him feel so incredible? he wondered. How could it wipe away years of loneliness and self-doubts? He didn't know the answer to that, but he did know that tonight had changed him. That *she* had changed him.

Since the lamp was still burning, the golden hue lit her face and gave her damp skin a pearlescent glow. A rosy tinge swept along her cheekbones and darkened her swollen lips. The lovely sight of her had him turning on his side and trailing his fingers across her forehead.

"It was very special for me, too," he murmured thickly.

Her lashes fluttered and she tilted a doubtful gaze up to his face. "You don't have to say that. I'm sure I must have seemed—well, very green."

He gave her a drowsy smile. "Hmm. Green is my favorite color. So don't change. Okay?"

She smiled back at him, then chuckled softly. "I'll try not to."

Sighing at the utter pleasure he was feeling at the moment, he gathered her close and buried his face in the side of her hair. "I feel like standing up and beating my fists against my chest," he admitted.

She groaned in protest. "Please don't do that. I don't want you to move. I want to keep you here just like this."

His arms tightened around her. "Don't worry. I'm not going anywhere. Not for a while, at least."

Russ didn't leave Laurel's bed, or her house, until the wee hours of the morning. By then it was snowing, and the ride to his own place was too short for the truck interior to warm. When he climbed between the cold sheets, he told himself he must have been crazy to get up and leave her. She hadn't asked him to. But after thinking it over, he decided it had been the right thing to do.

She'd just now learned what it was like to have sex with him. She needed time to get used to the idea of them being together as a couple before he started pushing his way into her private space and throwing the idea of love and marriage at her.

Love and marriage. He wasn't ashamed to admit that he was old-fashioned enough to believe the two things went hand in hand, that a man and a woman couldn't be truly together as one if they didn't have both entities binding them together.

But he had to admit to himself that the thought of love, marriage and Laurel had never crossed his mind at the same time. Separately perhaps, but never together. Oh, over the five years that she'd worked for him, he'd sometimes wondered if she'd ever loved a man, or had ever planned to marry. But the questions in his mind had been born from a general curiosity that one person has about another, not from a personal interest.

After all, for three years of those five, he'd had Brooke, and while they'd been married his affections had never strayed. He'd never thought of Laurel or any woman in a romantic way. And after Brooke was out of his life, he'd been too hurt and disillusioned to want a woman.

At work with Laurel, he'd always felt good and comfortable, as though she completed him. And away from work, well, he'd not thought much at all about being alone, living alone. He always had Laurel and work to go back to.

It had taken him two long years and a change in jobs for him to see that work without Laurel wouldn't be the same. Living without Laurel near him wouldn't be the same. And now, tonight, love had descended on him like an ominous cloud that he couldn't outrun.

I'm not sure I know what being in love is about.

Earlier tonight he'd tried to brush away Laurel's troubled statement. He'd not wanted to dwell on it or let the doubts of her words ruin the specialness of having her body close to his.

But now, as he lay alone in the cold darkness, he wondered if all of his newfound feelings were going to be unreturned, if finding real, true love was going to evade him a second time.

Much later, just as dawn was about to break over the mountaintops, Russ finally shut his mind down enough to drift into sleep. But the mental release came to an abrupt end when the cell on the nightstand rang loudly.

The moment he answered, Laramie's voice sounded

in his ear, "Russ, we have a cow trying to calve, but it's not going like it should. I don't think pulling is an option. You'd better come."

Instantly awake, Russ shoved back the covers and reached for his jeans. As he did, he heard a thump behind him and looked around to see he'd caused Leo to slip off the foot of the bed. The cat looked totally insulted, and Russ took a second to place the feline back on the cozy mattress.

"I'll be right there," he told the foreman. After jerking on the remainder of his clothes and boots, he headed out the door. On his way to the truck, he punched Laurel's number.

She answered on the second ring, and he could tell from her voice that she was already wide awake.

Not wasting words, she said, "I got the call, too. I'll be waiting at the gate."

Two minutes later, he skidded the truck to a halt and she quickly climbed in. Since snow was still continuing to fall at a heavy pace, she'd flipped the hood of her coat over her head. The furry edge shrouded most of her face from view, but the parts he could see looked pale and tired. He felt guilty about that. Very guilty.

"Did you get any sleep at all?" he asked.

"Maybe two hours. What about yourself?"

"Enough," he muttered.

The lights from the dashboard illuminated his profile, and as Laurel allowed her gaze to slide over his face, she decided he looked exhausted. Still, she'd seen him looking far worse, during some of those twenty-hour work marathons when he'd not stopped to eat or sleep. Loss of sleep because he'd been making love to her for most of the night was nothing compared to those times.

Is that what you're calling it, Laurel? Making love?

Why don't you face things as they really are. Russ had sex with you. Hot, wild sex. Love wasn't any part of it.

The taunting voice in her head made her jaw tighten and her eyes unexpectedly glaze with moisture. Long ago, after her mother had left the family, after watching her sister being lowered into the ground and her father and brother beating a hasty path away from her, Laurel had decided she wasn't going to invest her heart in a husband or children. Loving her family hadn't kept them with her or even made them love her back. It had only made her hurt worse when she'd finally lost them. She couldn't go through that agony again. Not for anything or anyone.

But, oh my, tonight, after she'd given herself to Russ, after she'd lain in his arms and felt his lips worshipping her body as though she were something precious to him, she'd been hit with a longing so deep that she was still aching from it. Even now, she wished things could be different, that she could be bold enough and confident enough to reach for the things that most women dream of—the love of a man and children from that love.

Shoving the impossible thoughts from her mind, she tried to focus on the issue at hand.

"You figure we're looking at a C-section?"

He nodded grimly. "'Fraid so. Let's just hope we've got enough time to save mother and calf."

The remainder of the short drive to the ranch was made in tense silence. At times like these, Russ was always preoccupied with the task ahead of them, and she understood he didn't need to be distracted with a bunch of small talk. Instead, she stared out the passenger window and wondered what this night was going to mean to them later on. Would it eventually draw them closer together or split them completely apart?

Chapter Eight

At the calving barn, she and Russ were met by Laramie and Seth, the manager of the calving operation of the Chaparral. A tall man with a lean, ruddy face, she gauged him to be somewhere in his mid to late thirties.

As the four of them quickly made their way toward the area of the barn where the cow was located, it was clear that neither Laramie or Seth was in a jovial mood.

"The heifer was way too young to be bred in the first place," Seth explained to Russ. "And the hell of it, we're expecting about thirty more of these early calves this winter."

"A downed fence allowed a bull into a section full of heifers," Laramie spoke up. "We still haven't figured out how that happened. The cowboys that found it swore it looked as though the wire had been cut, but hell, anything could have knocked it down."

"Yeah," Seth added, "and the mess it made is going to continue until all of these calves are born safely."

"At least we discovered the bull was misplaced before he got to the whole herd of heifers," Laramie said. "That's something to be thankful for."

"Well, let's hope most of them will calve without incident," Russ said in an effort to inject a note of optimism.

By now they'd reached the end of the barn, where the troubled cow was in a stall filled deep with straw. After Russ made a quick examination, he determined a C-section would have to be performed and instructed a few of the ranch hands who'd gathered around to move her to an enclosed area with a smooth concrete floor.

To Laurel's surprise, Maccoy was there and had already gathered all the medicine and tools necessary to treat a troubled birth. It was on the tip of her tongue to tell the older man it wasn't necessary for him to get out on a Sunday morning, especially when it was so cold and snowy. But she kept the comment to herself. Maccoy was a proud man and he wanted to feel as useful and needed as the next person, even if he was past his prime years. She only wished her own father could have been like Maccoy, ready and wanting to help. Instead, Nels had been too weak or uncaring—she'd never decided which—to offer any sort of care to his dying daughter.

Gathering up the tray of tools, she hurried over to where Russ was already kneeling over the bedded Angus cow. He immediately began to give her instructions, and she followed them by quickly filling two syringes with the correct dosage.

"Is the calf still alive?" she asked as she handed the medication to him.

Without delay, he administered the localized drug into the area where he'd be cutting. "It appears to be."

"You think she's been in labor for very long?" Something about seeing mother animals struggling to give birth always got to Laurel more than anything else she encountered in her job. She understood it was a part of nature and the cycle of life. But she was a woman, and in spite of her plans to remain childless, she could imagine their suffering, the fierce need to bear and protect their little ones.

"Yes. She's exhausted. But she'll be okay, I think."

Laurel didn't ask more. She'd been at the job long enough to know there were no certainties in cases like this, only gut feelings. And for the moment Laurel's feelings were twisted with worry. But she shoved them aside and focused on the task of helping Russ open the cow's womb.

As always, his hands worked quickly and precisely, and in a short amount of time he was pulling the calf away from its mother and onto the floor.

Next to him, Laurel was ready and waiting with a large sheet of absorbent muslin. He took it from her and immediately wiped the calf's nose and mouth, then paused as everyone in the room waited anxiously to hear it draw in a breath.

"Come on, little girl," he said to the lifeless calf. "You're out in the big world now. You've got to breathe for yourself now. Mama can't do it anymore."

The slick, wet calf made no sound or motion, and Russ gestured to Laurel. "I've got to close the mother up. Get the calf off the concrete and see if you can get any response from her."

Before any of the men could make a move, Laurel picked up the newborn calf and rushed to a nearby stall where a heater hanging from the rafters blew warm air into the small square of space covered with straw.

Even though Laurel's insides felt as if she were moving in a panicked rush, on the outside she managed to keep her ministrations smooth and deliberate as she massaged the heifer's tiny nostrils and pushed gently against her rib cage.

She had to live. She had to live.

The desperate mantra went over and over in Laurel's head as she worked frantically on the calf. The baby was her and Russ's first test on this ranch. Her survival represented everything that the two of them stood for.

"Breathe! Breathe!" Laurel whispered the command.

"Maa-oooo."

The sound was a weak cry, but it was a start. And then she saw the calf's rib cage suck in a deep, life-giving breath.

Overcome with relief, she practically sobbed. "That's it, girl! Keep going. You're fine now. Just fine."

Laurel watched the calf take several more breaths. When it began to kick and attempt to lift its head, its survival was apparent. As she went to work cleaning and drying the rest of the body, a spattering of cheers and claps sounded behind her, and she jerked her head around to see a few of the ranch hands had gathered at the opening of the stall.

Smiling, she gave them a thumbs-up sign just as Russ parted his way through the group of celebrating men and stepped into the stall.

As he joined her at the calf's side, Laurel smiled triumphantly up at him. "She's going to live."

"So is the mother. We'll get her set up with an IV and get her on her feet, then move her in here with her baby."

"What about her milk?" Laurel asked, knowing that

young mothers, especially after a difficult birth, sometimes had problems producing enough.

"Looks like she's going to have plenty. But we'll keep a watch on both of them for a few days before they're turned back out to pasture. We were lucky that the ranch hands were keeping a sharp eye and found her before it was too late."

Rising to her feet, she saw relief in his brown eyes and something else she couldn't quite define, something that said he wanted to pull her into his arms. The idea thrilled her, yet at the same time a tiny part of her wanted to scurry backward and away from the connection that seemed to be drawing them closer and closer together.

"The cowboys did a good job finding her, but without you here to treat her, the cow and calf would have perished," she pointed out.

A wry grin twisted his lips. "I'm not wearing an *S* on my chest or leaping over tall buildings in a single bound, Laurel. All I did was perform a plain and simple C-section that any decent vet could manage out in the pasture. Besides," he added in a voice lowered just for her. "I couldn't have done it without you. We're a good team."

He'd never praised her like this before. In fact, she'd always believed that he took her work for granted. Having him describe the two of them as a good team caught her completely off guard.

As she tried to decide how to respond to his compliment, a smile crept its way across her face.

"You're full of surprises, Dr. Hollister," she said finally.

"Yeah, sometimes I surprise myself."

The grin he shot her was a shade short of naughty

and something she'd never seen on him before. It drew her gaze straight to his lips and the glint of his white teeth, and suddenly all she could think about was the way he'd kissed and held her, the urgency and passion she'd experienced as he'd made love to her. Their time together had been so precious and wonderful. She was already dreaming of when it might happen again. Yet if she was smart, she wouldn't let herself fall into bed with this man a second time. Not if she wanted to keep her heart distanced from him.

At their feet, the calf struggled to rise on all fours. Grateful for the distraction, Laurel said, "She's ready to find her mother's milk. Think the cow can stand?"

"We'll help her," he said.

Nodding, she turned away from him to leave the stall, but quickly came to an abrupt stop as a light-headed feeling caused her to weave unsteadily on her feet.

Russ's hand shot out and swiftly caught her by the elbow in order to support her. "Laurel! Are you okay?"

Drawing in a shaky breath, she attempted to laugh it off. "I'm fine. My head just took a bit of a whirl for a moment. It's nothing."

As she passed trembling fingers over her forehead, she noticed that Laramie, Seth and Maccoy had entered the stall, along with a couple of ranch hands. All of them were wearing concerned looks, as though they expected her to collapse at any moment.

"Has Laurel hurt herself?" Laramie questioned.

Russ answered, "I don't know if—"

Laurel quickly interrupted, "I'm fine. Just a bit dizzy from being hungry. That's all."

"Well, that'll be easy enough to fix." Maccoy spoke up with a relieved grin. "When I left the bunkhouse a few minutes ago, the cook was stirring up a pan of biscuits. They ought to be ready right about now."

"We'll come over as soon as we finish up here," Russ told the older man.

Seeing that Laurel appeared to be standing on her own power, the men eased out of the stall. She started to follow, only to have Russ's hand tighten on her arm.

"Just a minute, Laurel. Are you sure you're okay? I've never seen you have a dizzy spell before. Even when we're working out in ninety-degree weather."

A blush suddenly stung her cheeks to a bright red. "That's because I—well, the two of us haven't exactly been sleeping all night. And I missed breakfast. You might be able to run on empty. But I'm not too good at it."

A look of dawning clicked in his eyes. "I wasn't thinking. I guess you have had an unusually taxing night. The next time we make love, I'll try to make sure we're not called out on emergency."

The next time. Now was the perfect moment for Laurel to tell him there wasn't going to be a next time. But she wasn't going to make promises she knew she couldn't keep. Besides being pointless, it would make it look as though her word was worthless.

"That would be helpful," she tried to joke.

With his hand still on her arm, he urged her out of the stall. "Let's go see if we can get mama standing."

Three days later, the month rolled into February. Laurel and Russ were so busy at work that she hadn't had much time to think about the dizzy spell she'd experienced in the calving barn. But at night, when quietness set in and her mind began to drift, the incident would creep back to haunt her. Light-headedness was one of the first symptoms that Lainey had displayed when she'd become ill.

No doctor had ever told Laurel that she would likely develop the same blood disorder that had claimed her twin's life. But on the other hand, no doctor had ever stepped out on a limb and assured her that she was safely immune to the disease.

The uncertainty was something Laurel had accepted and lived with all these years. And for the most part, she'd not gone around worrying that she too would become a victim of the disease. After all, there was no way a person could really live if he or she was preoccupied with dying. No, her worries had never dwelled upon her own health; they had always been about losing the people that she loved and cared about.

But now that she and Russ had gotten closer, the uncertainty of it all hit home even harder. What if she allowed herself to get closer to Russ? What if she actually let herself fall in love with him and then she became ill? No one had to tell her that he was a devoted man. If he committed himself to Laurel, he'd stay committed to the bitter end. Even if it meant hours of caretaking and giving up a normal life for himself.

There was no way she'd ever put him through that sort of hell. Besides, Russ was too good a man to be tied to a warped woman like her. He needed someone fresh and vibrant, someone with a sunny nature who would fill his home with kids and his life with love. Yes. That's what Russ deserved and that's what she wanted for him.

"You're awfully quiet over there," Russ commented as the old truck shook and rattled over a rutted track that barely resembled a road.

This morning the two of them were in one of the ranch's older trucks that were used for traveling over rough terrain. And Laurel could see the sturdy vehicle was definitely needed as they drove northward toward a range of mountains. In many places, the path they were traveling was washed out and often blocked with shifting rocks and clumps of brush. For the past ten minutes, Laurel had been gripping the armrest to keep her head from being tossed into the windshield.

"I'm too busy hanging on to try to talk," she told him. "It would help if this old thing had working seat belts. At least I could tie myself down."

Russ chuckled. "If it was good enough to have working seat belts, it would be too good to drive over this ground. But I don't think we'll have to go too much farther. From Laramie's directions, after we pass through this next gate we should find the herd close by."

Late yesterday evening, the foreman and some of the ranch hands had been riding this area and spotted a herd with a few cows that were displaying peculiar behavior. Now she and Russ were on their way to find the cattle and determine if some sort of contagious disease was starting to spread through them.

"We should have come by horseback," she said, her fingers gripping the edge of the frayed bench seat. "The ride certainly would have been smoother than this buckboard."

"Smoother, but much longer. And we don't have time to waste." He glanced curiously over at her. "Now that I think about it, I've never seen you on a horse. You've helped me treat hundreds of them over the years, but I didn't know you could ride."

"You never asked."

"That's why I'm asking now. I'm trying to learn more about you."

A hopeless feeling suddenly struck her, but she just

as quickly tried to shove it away. She enjoyed being with this man in any capacity. To dwell on what could or couldn't be would only ruin the pleasure she got from working at his side.

Shrugging, she said, "I wouldn't call myself an excellent horsewoman by any stretch of the imagination, but I can sit a saddle pretty well. My twin and I learned to ride when we were just little girls. A good friend of ours lived on a ranch with lots of horses. Her father was kind and patient enough to teach us."

"Is your friend still around?"

"No. Her folks sold the property and they moved to another ranch in Southern California. She's still lives there, and from time to time I get a card or call from her."

"So you quit riding after she left town?"

Laurel shook her head. "About the time she moved away, I'd gotten acquainted with Alexa and the two of us used to ride quite a bit. That was before—well, before Alexa left Lincoln County and went to work in Santa Fe."

"Was your sister still living then?"

She'd not been expecting that sort of question from him. In the years she'd known him, he'd rarely ever brought up the subject of her family, never pushed her to talk about her parents or siblings. But to be fair, when he'd owned the clinic in town, every minute of the day had been consumed with work and they'd not had much time for talk, unless it pertained to treating their patients. Maybe he'd wanted to ask her personal things, but there had never been an opportunity for it.

Laurel had certainly wanted to ask him things. Especially when he was going through his divorce. During that period, he'd lost weight and practically quit talking altogether. She'd wanted to yell at him and ask him if Brooke was worth ruining his health over. But she'd kept her comments and questions to herself. The last thing she'd wanted was for him to get the idea that she was jealous, that she cared about his welfare much more than Brooke ever had.

Releasing a long, heavy breath, she finally answered, "Lainey had already passed on by then. I was in high school and my father and brother were already making plans to move to Arizona."

A stretch of silence passed and Laurel could see from his expression that he was chewing thoughtfully on her words.

Eventually, he said, "The other day you told me that you didn't want to talk about your sister. And you don't have to now. I'm just wondering—you mentioned your father and brother, but not your mother. Was she not around?"

The morning sun was shining brightly and the sky was a picture-perfect azure-blue that could only be found in New Mexico. Yet the sunny sky couldn't push away the darkness of her memories.

"No. By then she'd been gone for a few years." Stiffening her spine, she swallowed hard, then turned slightly in the seat to face him. "You see, my mother, Stacie, left the family not long after my sister was diagnosed with the blood disorder that killed her."

He eased his foot off the accelerator and the truck's speed slowed to a crawl. "Left?" he asked, clearly dumbfounded. "Are you serious?"

Suddenly she was angry. Not at him, but at all the loss and misery her mother had caused the whole Stanton family. "Why would I make up something so awful? It's not like it's something I even want people to know.

That my mother was so worthless that she couldn't deal with a sick child. That she didn't have the gumption or the love to stick around and care for her own daughter!"

Unconsciously, her voice had risen with each word she'd spoken, and now as Russ stared at her, she realized she'd probably been close to shrieking. It wasn't like her to lose control of her emotions. And it certainly wasn't like her to let loose like this with Russ.

"I— Oh, God, I'm sorry," she apologized, her low voice full of regret. "It's not often that I ever say my mother's name. I get very angry when I talk about her."

Russ braked the truck to a halt and turned toward her. "I'm the one who's sorry, Laurel. I didn't have any idea that—well, now is not the time or place for this. When I asked—"

"Forget it, Russ. Is there ever a right time or place to talk about unpleasant memories?"

"No. I guess not." He shook his head. "I've always been curious as to why you never mentioned your mother. I even asked Maccoy once if he knew anything about your family."

Surprised by his admission, she stared at him. "Why didn't you ask me?"

He shrugged. "I don't know. You never asked me personal things, so I didn't want to come off as being the nosy one. But Maccoy couldn't tell me anything, except that your sister had died and your father and brother had moved away. So I took it for granted that your parents were divorced or something and she wasn't around."

Laurel let out a bitter laugh. "Divorced? I guess so. I never really knew what happened legally with my parents. You see, they never had a strong marriage. There was always bickering going on. Even if the situation hadn't occurred with Lainey, they would have probably divorced, I can see that now. Serious problems either pull people together or push them apart. Now I have no idea if my mother is still living. Once she left, that was it."

He looked away from her and across a small meadow that was covered with patches of snow. Laurel wondered what he was thinking. That she came from a mess of a family? That her bad genes made her a risky partner to work with, to love?

"What kind of person was she?" Russ asked. "Did you love her?"

A ball of emotion suddenly filled her throat. She tried to clear it away, but her voice sounded raspy when she spoke. "I believe you're the first person who's ever asked me that question, Russ. No one else seemed to ever care or wonder if I loved my mother, or if her leaving had hurt me. I guess they were all too busy worrying over Lainey. And rightly so. Her health was more important than my state of mind. But to answer your question, yes, I loved my mother. When she went away it was like my whole world collapsed. My father and brother were pretty useless. So it was mainly just me and my sister. Me caring for her and her clinging to me."

"I see."

She grimaced. "How could you possibly see?"

"I'll tell you how later," he said with a grim frown. "Right now we'd better head on up the mountain and find that herd of cows."

Normally Laurel would have been relieved that she no longer had to talk about private issues, but as Russ put the truck back in motion, she felt strangely deflated. Talking to him about her past hadn't felt degrading. She'd wanted to tell him more, to let that horrible dam inside her break and let every dark thought and fear come tumbling out.

That's because you're changing, Laurel. That's because sharing that part of yourself has started to feel natural and right. Just like making love to him had felt good and right.

While she mulled over her thoughts, he put the truck back into forward motion. They traveled a quarter mile before a wide galvanized fence blocked the roadway. Past it, the track turned between two low hills, then climbed until another mountain meadow appeared.

"There they are," Russ announced as he spotted the cattle.

About forty head of black Angus were gathered near a lone tree at the back side of the opening. As soon as they noticed the approaching truck, the cattle's heads came up and several of them began trotting toward them.

Russ quickly parked the truck in the middle of the road. "Let's spread the feed and try to look them over as they eat," he told Laurel.

In a matter of minutes the whole herd had wandered up to partake of the range cubes that Russ had poured onto the ground. All except eight of the cows were eating heartily, and those eight were standing to one side, bawling lowly.

"Look, Russ, that one isn't walking quite right. She's staggering! Maybe they have blackleg or listeriosis."

"Those things do make it tough for a cow to walk. And anything is possible, but God help us if it is a problem coming from the soil. Let's try to get a closer look at them," he told her.

In the past, whenever they were called out to an area ranch, they tended cattle or animals that were already penned. It wasn't very often that they dealt with cows or bulls out in the open without a chute or corral to confine them. And even then, they had cowboys there to rope and secure the cattle. In this case, Russ could only observe from a distance, or at best, try to get a hands-on look.

A few minutes later, Russ and Laurel walked a short distance away from the cattle and over to the side of the truck. "Laramie's hunch was right. The cows are sick," Russ said. "But with what I'm not sure yet. I think we can rule out blackleg. I didn't see any swelling. But that's just one of many things that could be wrong."

Laurel had learned a lot over the years she'd worked as Russ's assistant. He didn't have to tell her that there was a list of cattle diseases as long as her arm, and some of them were difficult to diagnose. He'd need to do extensive blood work and examinations to determine exactly what was affecting these particular cows.

Pulling out a cell phone, he made a quick call to Laramie. Once he hung up, he said to Laurel, "They'll be here as soon as they gather up panels and a truck and trailer. A couple of cowboys on horseback are coming too, just in case some of the sick cattle bolt and need to be rounded up. I told Laramie we'd stay put, just in case we're needed here."

She opened the truck door. "Why don't we get back inside and have a cup of coffee," Laurel suggested. "There's not anything we can do standing out here in the cold."

Early this morning, while Russ had been gathering tools and medications, Laurel had filled a thermos with hot coffee and thrown a few snacks into a sack. Now as they settled themselves back on the bench seat, she pulled out two foam cups and poured each of them half full.

"I brought candy and cookies," she offered.

A faint grin touched his lips. "You came prepared, did you?"

She pulled an oatmeal cookie from a small plastic container. "After that dizzy spell the other night, I'm not going to take any chances."

His grin dissolved as he looked over at her. "Has that happened anymore?"

"No. Not at all. Why do you ask? You can see for yourself that I'm fine."

He reached over and slid his fingers over the back of her hand. "I can't do all this work without you," he softly teased.

It was the first time since the night they'd made love that he'd initiated any sort of flirtation, and though it was a ridiculous reaction, she was suddenly struck with shyness.

Staring down at the sack on her lap, she quipped, "I'll make sure to eat a few more cookies."

Placing his coffee cup on the dashboard, he scooted over on the bench seat until his shoulder was touching hers. The contact set Laurel's heart on a runaway pace.

"That's what I like about these old vehicles," he said lowly. "There's no console or bucket seats to keep me from getting close to you."

She twisted her face around to his. "What are you doing over here?" she asked inanely.

"You need to ask? Ever since I left your bed the other night, I've been dying to get close to you again."

She nervously licked her lips and reminded herself to breathe. "You've had plenty of opportunities. We live within walking distance of each other."

"That's true. But these past few nights I've been tied up with stacks of paperwork. Most of it to do with tying up loose ends with Dr. Brennan and the clinic back in town." His fingertips gently grazed her cheek. "Besides, I felt like you needed time to think."

"About what?" she dared to ask.

"About me. And you. Together. Have you been thinking about us?"

The emotions he invoked in her were so full and overwhelming, all she could do was groan with dismay and bury her face against his shoulder.

"That's all I've been able to think about, Russ."

"And?"

"I've always abhorred the idea of having an affair. And I never thought I'd be the kind of woman who'd ever agree to have one. But I want you, Russ. I'm not going to waste time trying to deny it."

He said nothing and then his hands were unexpectedly lifting her head away from his shoulder. As he carefully studied her face, Laurel felt her cheeks grow red-hot.

"An affair?" he whispered in disbelief. "That's what you think I want?"

The trembling going on inside her moved outward, forcing her to grip the front of his jacket to keep her hands from visibly shaking. "That's what I assumed. I'm sorry if I misunderstood and jumped to conclusions. From the way you're looking at me, I can only guess that I'm going way too fast for you. But after the other night—"

"Fast! Hellfire, Laurel, you don't know me at all! After all these years of working with me, where would you get the idea that I'm the sort of man who'd want to have an affair? Especially with a woman like you!"

Easing back, she glared at him. "What does that mean, a woman like me?"

"It means you're better than that."

Totally confused now, she said, "I'm sorry, Russ, but I don't understand. If you don't want us to be that close—then what do you want?"

Sighing with frustration, he wiped a hand over his face. "Oh, Laurel, are you really that clueless? Can't you see that I love you? I want you to be my wife."

Never in her life had she expected those words to come out of his mouth. And she had no doubt the shock must have shown on her face. "No—that can't be."

His hands reached for her shoulders and Laurel instinctively scooted away from him, until her back was pressed against the truck door.

"Laurel, I'm sorry. I didn't mean to blurt this out to you now. Especially here on the job like this. But now that I have—"

She interrupted the rest of his words with a violent shake of her head. "I wasn't expecting anything like this from you, Russ. It's not what I want!"

"Why?"

"Why?" she repeated blankly, then rolled her eyes with exasperation. "The reasons are too many to count!"

His nearness made the small interior of the cab seem even more confining. The need to escape took hold of her and she hastily reached for the door handle and jerked it open.

Before he could stop her, she practically leaped to the ground, then stumbled to the back of the truck. With her hands braced on the edge of the tailgate, she bent her head and drew in deep breaths of cold air.

But all too soon, she heard the truck door opening

and closing and then Russ's hands were on her shoulders, urging her to turn and face him.

"I don't want a list, Laurel," he said. "Just give me one good reason why you don't want more than an affair."

Blinking at the hot moisture in her eyes, she whirled on him. "Did you ever stop to consider that I might not love you?"

His solemn expression didn't flinch or change in any way. "I considered the possibility. But I'm betting that you do. You're not the type to give yourself to a man just for the sake of having sex. I may not know your favorite color or movie, or the way you like your eggs cooked. In fact, there's a hell of a whole lot I don't know about you. But I do know you wouldn't have given your virginity to a man you didn't care about."

Tight-lipped, she looked at him and wondered why she was shaking, why she desperately felt like bursting into tears. The man she'd idolized for so long had just proposed to her. Not only that, he'd vowed his love. Any other woman would be deliriously happy. But to Laurel, her greatest fears had finally caught up to her and now they were slapping her in the face.

"My virginity," she muttered with sarcasm. "Don't let that go to your head. Love had nothing to do with that. I'm thirty years old. I just decided it was time to see what all the fuss was about."

She'd not only disgusted him, she failed to convince him. "You're a hell of a bad liar, Laurel. Don't even try."

Bending her head, she squeezed her eyes shut. "Okay, so I'm lying. But I meant what I said about the rest. If you don't want to have an affair with me, then you might as well forget it!"

"I'm not going to forget anything. And I'm not going to let you forget anything, either!"

She opened her mouth to counter his heated promise, but he didn't give her the chance to speak. Instead, he jerked her forward and into his arms.

"Russ—"

"You've already said too much. Way too much."

The hoarsely whispered words fanned her cheeks just before his lips settled hotly over hers.

All of her plans to be a strong woman dissolved as his kiss began to melt her like a patch of snow beneath a scorching-hot sun. It was scandalous the way his body affected hers, the way it swept her mind of everything but him. Before she could think or stop herself, her arms circled around his neck, her lips opened beneath his.

The wind was cold against her face and, off to their right, she could hear cows milling around the creep feed. Birds twittered around them and the breeze whispered a song in the nearby pines. The sound and scents swirled around her, mixing with the euphoria his lips were creating.

Laurel was so lost she didn't catch the far-off sound of an approaching vehicle until it was almost upon them. And even then she didn't want to acknowledge the interruption. Thankfully, Russ had enough willpower to lift his head and promptly set her away from him.

"The men are coming," he said gruffly. "We'll finish this later—tonight."

"Yes, we'll definitely finish this," she muttered, then before he could see the sting of moisture in her eyes, she whirled her back to him and fought to compose herself.

Finish. How ironic that Russ had been the one to throw that word at her, she thought sickly. Because she was the one who would have to finish everything between them and put an end to his crazy notion about marriage. Most of all, she was going to have to go against everything her heart was telling her and convince him, once and for all, that she didn't love him.

Chapter Nine

That night Russ was in the kitchen, seasoning steaks to put on the grill when Quint called with questions regarding the sick cattle. As usual the ranch owner was easy to talk to, even when he was concerned about something. That was one of the things that Russ liked best about Quint. The man had money to burn, he didn't need to work to provide his family with a lavish lifestyle. But he wasn't about either of those things. He was a regular Joe whose life was dedicated to his family's ranches and the people he loved.

"Right now Laurel and I are treating their symptoms," he told Quint. "That's really all I can do until I determine exactly what's wrong. The preliminary blood tests I ran today were inconclusive. I've sent more samples to NMU in Las Cruces. They tell me it might take two weeks before they get the results."

"Damn, every cow on the place could be dead by then," Quint muttered.

"Sometimes these things take a while," Russ explained. "Especially if cultures have to be grown."

"Yeah, I understand. It's just so frustrating. And I'm concerned this stuff might sweep through the rest of that particular herd. Or even jump to the other herds on the ranch. Is that possible? It seems odd that only eight of them showed signs of being sick."

"I wish I could give you guarantees that it won't spread, Quint. But I can't without knowing what I'm dealing with. I'm sure Laramie has already told you he's instructed the men to keep a daily watch on the affected herd. As it stands, I've checked with all the area vets—they're not seeing this problem. At least, not yet. So it seems isolated to the Chaparral. Right now it's wait and see."

Quint cursed under his breath. "Well, that's just the way the cards are dealt sometimes. What about these eight? Do you think you can save them?"

"Two of them are in bad condition. We'll have to see how they fare in the next twenty-four hours. The rest of them are already showing signs of improvement, so that's encouraging. As for the calves they're carrying, I can't give you a prognosis yet."

After blowing out a long breath, Quint said, "Well, there's no need for me to ask—I already know you'll do your best with the situation. It's definitely not a problem I'd wish on the Chaparral or any other ranch. But I'm damned glad you're there to handle this."

Quint's vote of confidence made Russ feel a tad better, but on the other hand it put an even greater burden on his shoulders. If he didn't deal with this problem quickly and efficiently, he was going to appear worthless to the ranch.

"I won't stop until the problem is fixed," he assured the other man.

Their conversation moved on to more general issues of the Chaparral's livestock before Quint finally announced that he needed to end the call. With the phone connection ended, Russ tossed his cell onto the end of the cabinet and went back to preparing the remainder of the meal.

As he tossed the steaks on the indoor grill, he glanced at his watch. Laurel was usually prompt, so he had ten minutes to finish cooking everything before she arrived.

This afternoon, when the two of them had finally gotten caught up with treating the cattle and quarantining them away from the other animals at the ranch yard, Russ had taken Laurel aside and invited her to have supper with him.

After the mess he'd made of things this morning, he'd wanted to take Laurel to town for dinner tonight to a special place where he'd hoped to make her feel pampered and appreciated. But she'd nixed that idea before he could hardly get the suggestion out of his mouth. She didn't want him making a big deal over anything, she informed him. All she wanted this evening was a simple snack and a few minutes of talk.

Well, she was going to get more than she'd asked for, he thought.

At the same time, a short distance down the mountain, in her own house, Laurel stood in front of the dresser mirror and wondered what in heck she thought she was doing. This evening with Russ was only going to be a simple snack followed with a talk. That was all she'd agreed to! So what had she been thinking when she'd pulled on a long, gray woolen skirt and a black, form-fitting top?

Because for once in her life, she wanted to look like a woman, feel like a woman. Even if she had to end things with the man, she didn't want to do it looking as if she'd just walked out of a muddy cow lot.

Trying not to let herself dwell on the word *end,* she brushed through her long hair and pinned the top half up and back from her face with a rhinestone clasp. After dabbing perfume on her pulse points, she pulled on a long coat and, checking to make sure the cats had plenty of food and fresh water, she hurried out the door.

The night was cold, even for February in southern New Mexico, but thankfully the climb up the mountain to Russ's house was so short she didn't have time to shiver.

Since they'd moved to the Chaparral, she'd not visited his home. For the past three days, she'd certainly considered the idea several times. But after the night they'd spent in her bed, she'd figured if she showed up on his doorstep, he'd only think she was asking for another round of lovemaking.

So isn't he going to think that tonight, Laurel? You're dressed like a woman and smell like a woman. And your heart is certainly beating like that of a woman who wants her man. Do you honestly think the guy is going to believe you're there to end things?

Shaking away the doubtful voice in her head, she braked her truck to a stop a few feet from where Russ's truck was parked beneath a canopy connected to the side of the house. It didn't have to be the end, she told herself. Not completely. If she could make him see that a casual affair was all the two of them needed to be happy.

* * *

Russ was putting the final touches to the dining table, when he heard Laurel's knock on the front door and went to answer it.

"Come in, Laurel," he invited as he pushed the door wide. "Everything is ready."

She stepped into the house, suspiciously sniffing the air as she went. "I smell something cooking. You promised we'd have sandwiches, Russ."

Resting a hand against her back, he ushered her down a short entryway and then into a spacious living room with a dark maroon couch and two large stuffed armchairs done in navy blue. A rock fireplace, much larger than the one in her house, stretched across the far southern wall. A fire hissed and crackled, filling the space with welcome warmth.

"I decided I didn't want sandwiches tonight. But be warned, my cooking can't be compared to Reena's."

"You shouldn't have cooked at all," she said. "I told you not to."

"I don't always do what you tell me to do," he challenged.

"You never do what I tell you to do," she pointed out.

He moved his hands to her shoulders and she stopped in her tracks, tensed and poised as though she might need to run at any given moment. Her guarded behavior didn't surprise Russ. Ever since he'd blurted out that he wanted to marry her, she'd taken a sudden and drastic turn away from him. All through the day, she'd gone out of her way to keep a safe distance between them, and now he could feel the awkward barrier she was still trying to hold between them.

"Let me hang your coat here in the closet," he said quietly. "Are you warm enough? I turned up the heat after I got home this evening, but the weather is beginning to get nasty out there."

As the coat slid off her shoulders, he caught the soft scent of roses and the smell drew him back to the night he'd taken her to bed. Her skin had felt as smooth as flower petals beneath his lips and had tasted even sweeter.

"It feels nice in here, thank you."

After dealing with her coat, he turned back to her and was very nearly blown away at the sight. Without the coat, he could see she'd dressed in a long woolen skirt that gently draped her curves. A black ribbed top was tucked into the waist and belted with a soft black ribbon. With her hair pulled back, it made her cheekbones stand out and her luminous gray eyes more prominent. He'd never seen her looking so lovely or more womanly, and it was all he could do to keep from pulling her into his arms right then and there.

But he'd already tried that tactic this morning and in the end it hadn't worked, he reminded himself. Tonight he couldn't let the desire that was slowly simmering in his loins take complete control. Not until he'd persuaded her to marry him.

At the moment, her attention had strayed from him and over to the living room. As she regarded her surroundings with interest, it dawned on Russ that she'd not yet seen his house.

"I'll show you around the place after we eat," he promised. "Right now the food is ready and I don't want it to get cold."

"Fine. I am hungry," she agreed. "And whatever you've made smells good."

With his hand on her upper arm, he guided her toward the dining room. "You're about to find out if it tastes good."

* * *

Being alone with Russ, under any circumstances, was a risky venture. This morning had certainly proved that, Laurel thought grimly. Now, as he led her into a cozy dining room situated just off the kitchen, she realized she'd made a giant mistake in agreeing to come here tonight. For some reason, the simple snack he'd promised had turned into a candlelight dinner for two.

"Russ—what is this?" she asked, staring skeptically at the table. "And where did you get those flowers?"

"Don't worry about where I got the flowers. I have my sources," he told her smugly. "So just enjoy them."

He pulled out a chair for her. "Make yourself comfortable and I'll go fetch the rest of our meal."

Once he'd seated her in the chair and left the room, Laurel stared around in stunned fascination at a bottle of wine and an accompanying pair of long-stemmed glasses, along with a huge bouquet of cut white daisies, pink mums and purple hyacinth. There were matching place mats and napkins, heavy silverware elaborately carved with decoration and china edged with a pattern of delicate roses. He'd clearly pulled out the special stuff tonight. And why? For her?

This morning he'd said that he loved her. Laurel had tossed his words around in her head all day and she was no closer to believing them now than she had been this morning. True, he'd taken her to bed, but that fact hardly spelled love. Now he'd cooked dinner for her. A seduction tactic, no doubt, she thought dismally. Even so, no man had ever gone to this much trouble to garner her attention, and that in itself softened her heart.

"I hope you like steak and potatoes, because that's what we're having."

She looked up to see him carrying two platters to

the table. Mouthwatering smells emanated from both dishes. "I think by now you know that I'm not a picky eater. It will be good, I'm sure."

He opened the wine bottle and after pouring their glasses half-full, took a seat kitty-corner to her right elbow. As they filled their plates with Caesar salad, he told her about Quint's call and the concerns the ranch owner had about the sick cattle.

This afternoon as the two of them had treated the animals, Laurel had sensed an urgency in Russ that she'd never seen in him before. She wasn't sure if it was the uncertainty of the illness or the fact that this change in jobs was requiring him to prove his qualities as a vet all over again. Either way, she hated to think of this strong man losing his confidence.

"You'll get it figured out, Russ. And when we left the barn this evening, the cattle appeared to be improving. So as far as treatments go, you're on the right track."

"Let's hope so," he replied.

Tonight he was wearing a dark green button-down shirt with the sleeves rolled back against his forearms. The color gave his tanned complexion a rich, golden hue and made his brown eyes even browner. Just looking at him very nearly took her breath.

If he decided to touch her, kiss her as he had this morning, she didn't know where she'd find the strength to resist. But she had to resist, she told herself. At least, until she made her feelings about their relationship clear to him.

"I didn't know you could cook," she said after she'd eaten a few bites of salad. "Did your ex-wife teach you?"

He barked out a dry laugh. "Brooke cook? She wasn't home long enough to boil water, much less make a meal. Actually, I'm not sure if she could cook. We usually ate takeout. Or something from a can or box. She was always busy at the investment firm where she worked, and I was usually at the clinic. Most of our meals were eaten on the fly."

"Oh. You make it sound like you and she were rarely ever together. How did you stay married for as long as you did?"

"Maybe that's why we did make it for as long as we did. We weren't in each other's faces."

"Like us, you mean?"

He looked at her, and her heart jumped at the suggestive glint she saw in his eyes.

"Yeah. Like us," he replied, then reached for his wineglass and took a long sip.

Laurel tried not to notice how the candlelight turned his skin to bronze and etched seductive shadows across his masculine features. She wasn't here to be seduced—she was here to state her case, she tried to remind herself.

"When I first started work at the clinic, I remember thinking you couldn't have much time to spend with your wife. Some nights we didn't leave there until ten or later."

With his attention on his plate, he said, "She didn't mind. I was making money and a name for myself. She had great aspirations for me in that way. Besides, she had other things to occupy her time. Like a coworker," he added caustically.

His statement took Laurel by complete surprise. With her fork paused in midair, she stared at him. "You mean another man?"

The corners of his mouth turned downward. "I figured you already knew about Brooke's straying affections. Maccoy did."

"Maccoy doesn't gossip. And neither do I."

"No. That's one thing I can say about you, Laurel. You've never pried into my personal life or anyone else's that I can see. I used to think you were indifferent—that you didn't care about people, because you never talked about them or asked questions. Later on, I decided you weren't indifferent—you were just a private person and wanted to be considerate of everyone else's privacy."

"I'm glad you figured that out. Because I do care about people. But sometimes—well, sometimes it hurts to have someone pry into things you don't want to talk about."

"That's true. But sometimes it helps." Seeing she was nearly finished with her salad, he pushed the meat and scalloped potatoes toward her. "As for me being able to cook, I learned how to get around in the kitchen a long time ago, when I was just a boy."

She smiled at him. "I can't imagine you being 'just a boy.'"

His lips took on a wry twist. "Guess you've always pictured me big and bossy."

"In a way." She placed a tiny bite of steak in her mouth. Once she'd chewed and swallowed, she looked at him in surprise. "This is delicious, Russ. Really."

"Thanks. I'm glad you like it. My culinary skills are a little rusty. I mostly eat something frozen or out of a can."

She sliced off another bite of the rare meat. "You say your learned how to cook when you were a boy. Who taught you? Your mother or dad?"

He ladled meat and potatoes onto his plate. "Curt Hollister and my mother divorced when I was about five years old. I've only see him once or twice since then. Not long after they split, he showed up to collect all his personal belongs. The second time was at my mom's funeral. So to answer your question—my dad didn't teach me anything. Except what not to be."

It felt odd, even jarring, hearing him reveal such things about his childhood. For some reason, she'd never imagined Russ coming from a broken family. He was too grounded and successful, too normal. "Oh, my. How much time had passed when you finally saw him at your mother's funeral services?" Laurel asked curiously.

"About twelve years. And during those years, my mother and I didn't have a clue as to where he'd gone. Actually, I don't think she wanted to know. Anyway, I was surprised when he showed up to pay his respects. I'm not even sure who'd contacted him about her death. My uncle, I'm guessing. In any case, it made me wonder if the man might have cared for his ex-wife after all."

On that one occasion in the past, Russ had mentioned his mother, but he'd never talked about his father and Laurel had assumed the man was either dead or had never been in the family circle. From what he was telling her now, she could understand why.

"Did you talk with him? Ask him anything?"

"We spoke briefly. By then I was seventeen and a whole lot resentful at his leaving. I didn't question him about his feelings toward my mother—she was gone and it all seemed pointless somehow."

She shook her head as she tried to imagine him dealing with losing his mother and confronting a father he never really knew, all at the same time. "So when your mom died, did your father ask you to go live with him?"

"He asked. But it was just a token offer," he said bitterly. "The man was a stranger. Up until then, he'd never made an attempt to see his son. He knew there wasn't any chance of me accepting his invitation. I think he wanted to appear loving and generous, but it was clear to me that the gesture was empty as a beggar's pockets."

"I see."

"No. You couldn't see. The man—" Suddenly he broke off and the embittered expression on his face turned to something like regret. "I'm sorry, Laurel. I started to say the man wasn't around to give me any sort of support while my mother was dying of cancer. But I can't tell you anything about being abandoned by a parent. Not after what you told me this morning about your mother."

Feeling closer to him than she'd ever imagined possible, she reached over and touched her hand to his. "I didn't have any idea, Russ. I've always imagined you coming from one of those perfect families like you see on those old television shows in the 1950s. With everyone loving each other, and the mishaps that did happen were minor ones. And even those drew everybody together."

"Those shows were fantasy."

Disappointed by his remark, she looked at him. "You sound so cynical."

He arched a brow at her. "And you're not? I'd think you'd be the first person to agree with me."

She shrugged. "Not really. I mean—yes, they were fantasy as far as my family. But I've always believed and hoped that there's something better out there than what I had. Than what you had."

"Fairy-tale families are for books and TV. But I do think there's something better out there, Laurel. Even after the ordeal I went through with Brooke, I still believe in love and children."

And that was more than she believed in, Laurel

thought sadly. So what did that make her, even more cynical than Russ? The idea troubled her.

"For you, Russ. Not for me."

"That doesn't make sense. But I'm not going to ask you to explain now. I'd rather we finish our meal first—before I start stating my case."

His forewarning put a lump in Laurel's throat and robbed her of most of her appetite, but she did her best to swallow down a good-size portion of meat and potatoes, along with a half glass of wine, before finally laying her fork aside.

"That was delicious, but I couldn't eat another bite," she said as she leaned back in her chair.

"What about cake and coffee? It's Italian cream."

She groaned with temptation. "Okay. But only a wee slice," she told him. So much for gulping down a sandwich and telling him that marriage was out of the question, she thought helplessly.

"Why don't you go on out to the living room, and I'll bring everything in there," he suggested.

"I should help you clear the table first."

"Forget it. I'll deal with the mess later."

Maybe it would be better if she went on out to the living room, she decided. Working beside him at the kitchen sink could lead to something she might not be able to resist.

"All right," she told him. "I'll go soak up some of that luscious heat from the fireplace."

Out in the other room, Laurel did go straight to the fireplace, but after warming her back for a few moments, curiosity got the better of her and she began to stroll around the room.

Behind the couch, and next to a floor-length window, bookshelves were built into the wall. She studied some of the titles and was wondering if or when he ever had time to read them when she noticed a small photo album jammed between two hardbacks.

Normally she wouldn't have dreamed of looking at such a personal item. But Russ had asked her to marry him. Didn't that mean he wanted to share his life with her? Even his past life?

Expecting to see images of him and his ex-wife, she was surprised to open the pages and find pictures of a woman and young boy. This had to his mother, Laurel thought, as she stared at the image of the dark-haired woman and the young boy standing next to her.

"That's a few snapshots of me and my mother."

The sound of Russ's voice brought Laurel's head up, and she found herself blushing as he entered the room with a tray of coffee and cake.

"I'm sorry. I hope you don't mind me looking."

"Not at all. I cherish that album. Those few images of her are the only ones I have. We didn't exactly have money to spend on cameras or film, and that was long before the days of digital images."

Laurel's gaze returned to the photos in her hands. "Your mother was very beautiful. Mine was, too," she said, unaware of the wistful note in her voice. "Was yours nice? What was her name?"

He placed the tray on a nearby end table, then walked over to her side. "Her name was Nanette," he said, "but most everyone called her Nan. As soon as she learned I wanted to be a vet, she was always encouraging me to follow my dreams."

A smile curved the corners of Laurel's lips. "And when was that?"

"Oh, probably by the time I was eight years old. I wanted to treat every wounded animal I found on the street or around town. Birds, cats, dogs, reptiles, whatever, they all fascinated me."

"I wish she could see you now," Laurel said softly. "See what a successful vet you've become."

He let out a quiet sigh. "Yeah, me, too. When she came down with cancer, I was devastated. I had no father. No siblings. She was my whole family." He drew in a long breath and let it out. "Back then I was afraid to go to bed at night. Afraid if I went to sleep I'd wake up and she'd be gone."

Laurel had felt the same sort of fear over Lainey. She'd been afraid to go to school, afraid to leave the house in case her sister should slip away from her. To think that Russ had experienced the same sort of fear was so difficult for her to imagine. He was always such a strong, steady rock, even when they were facing a dire emergency and an animal's life was in his hands. He never wavered or fell apart. He never showed a speck of fear. But he wasn't that vulnerable boy now. He was a grown man with the courage of a lion.

"So where did your uncle live? The one you went to after Nanette died?"

"Albuquerque. At seventeen, I thought I was old enough to take care of myself. I didn't want to move up there with him. But about the time Mom died, the bank was foreclosing on our house. I had nowhere else to stay."

Feeling foolish and small, Laurel closed the photo album and placed it back on the shelf. "I can't imagine that, Russ. Forgive me if this sounds insulting, but I've always assumed you'd come from a privileged family. You've always had so much and—"

"Laurel, before I met you I had worked as a vet for several years. I'd had time to accumulate what you're calling wealth. But I don't think I've ever been truly wealthy. Not with the things I consider a man's treasure."

She didn't ask him what he meant by that. She was afraid he would start talking about love, a wife and children. All the things she couldn't give him. Well, maybe she was capable of trying to give him those things, being those things for him, she thought. But Russ deserved more than "trying." He deserved a woman who understood what love meant, a woman who wouldn't be afraid to be a mother to his children, a wife who could handle the ups and downs of marriage. Not a woman who'd grown up without much love or guidance in her life.

She moved around the end of the couch and picked up a serving of cake and a coffee mug from the tray. As she carried it over to the fireplace, she said, "It's strange, isn't it, that we never knew these things about each other until now?"

He helped himself to the coffee and dessert, then moved across the room to where she stood on the hearth. "Before now we've never had the time to get to really know each other. Or the time to become close," he said in a low, husky voice.

She lowered herself to the warm rock hearth and made herself comfortable by settling her weight on one hip and drawing her legs around to one side.

"Being busy isn't the only reason," she said, as she carefully set her coffee cup on the hearth. "We've worked together for five years—long hours every day. But we had some quiet times, too. I don't think—well, at first you were married. And then later, after your divorce, you weren't exactly a happy man. Instead of talking to people, you barked."

"Back then I was feeling pretty worthless. I wasn't in any shape to contribute to a conversation."

Glancing up at him, she said, "Losing your wife must have devastated you. I guess you loved her very much."

Seemingly uninterested in his dessert, he placed the dishes on the fireplace mantel, then eased himself down to the hearth and settled close to her side. As his shoulder pressed into hers, Laurel felt her heart skip, then resume with a rapid thud.

"I once believed I loved Brooke more than anything. But that was in the beginning. After a while, I realized I'd married her for all the wrong reasons."

Completely surprised by his admission, she studied his face. "What does that mean? A man like you—I'm sure you married her for all the traditional reasons. And those couldn't be wrong."

One corner of his mouth lifted to a wry slant. "I was wrong to expect tradition out of someone who had no wish to conform. Brooke wasn't a family-type person. At least, not with me. I should have been smart enough to see that beforehand. Instead she made a fool of me. And it's taken a damned long time for me to realize I wasn't the inadequate one. She was."

Inadequate. Oh, God, couldn't Russ see that she, too, was lacking, Laurel wondered. And no matter how much she loved and wanted him, she needed to consider his happiness first. He'd already been hurt by one flawed woman. He didn't need a second one ruining his life all over again.

"You couldn't have guessed she would be unfaithful to you, Russ. And she probably didn't set out to be. People—well, some people are weak."

"Or selfish."

Forking a nibble of cake to her mouth, Laurel wondered what she could possibly say to that. Brooke probably had been selfish. But Laurel was in no position to judge the woman. She'd been accused of being selfish herself. Especially by Alexa, who believed Laurel should be sharing her love with a husband and children.

Suddenly Laurel's thoughts swung to her mother. Had she been wrong to judge her mother all these years? A crushing load had been thrown on Stacie Stanton's shoulders, and she'd been too emotionally weak to carry the burden of a dying child and a whining, dependent husband. She'd run away because she couldn't cope.

But her mother could have returned at some point, Laurel thought sadly. Or, at the very least, tried to contact her daughters again. As it stood, Laurel didn't have any idea where the woman was or what might have happened to her.

All these years, she'd told herself she didn't care that her mother had run away. "Good riddance to bad rubbish" was the motto Laurel had clung to. But now that she'd fallen in love and had given herself to Russ, it had shown her a myriad of feelings she'd never known existed. She could now see that life wasn't as simple as love or hate, black or white; there was so much more in between to consider.

Pushing her conflicting thoughts aside, Laurel asked, "Why did you call Brooke selfish?"

"Because she wanted everything her way."

"And you didn't? Want everything your way, that is."

Blowing out a long breath, he lifted his eyes toward the ceiling. "Maybe you could have called me selfish, too," he admitted. "I'm not sure anymore if she was more to blame for our failed marriage or if it was me. I only know we both messed up."

He squared around toward her, and Laurel's heart

swelled at the tenderness on his face, the softness in his eyes. This gentler, sweeter Russ was someone she'd never seen while they'd been in town at the clinic. And she still wasn't sure what had caused the change in him or even how to react to it.

"I don't want that to happen to you and me, Laurel," he said lowly. "I want us to be open and honest and sharing with each other. I want us to have children together, grow old together and be proud of the family we'll have to carry on our legacy."

With only half of her cake eaten, she placed her dishes behind her. "You make it all sound wonderful, Russ. But how could it ever possibly work? You and I— we've never belonged to a real family."

"That doesn't mean we can't make one of our own."

While Laurel was silently screaming at herself to move away from him, to garner enough space and strength to explain that she didn't want to give him children or be his wife, he reached for her and like a willing prey to a stalking cat, she waited for him to pull her into his captive embrace.

"Oh, Russ, if you really believe that, then you need to open your eyes. You need to see I'd make an even worse wife than Brooke."

A confused frown creased his face. "I don't understand why you'd think such a thing. But you're so wrong, sweet darling. So very wrong. And I'm willing to take the risk to prove that to you."

No! Even as his head drew closer and his mouth settled over hers, that one word was clanging like an alarm in her head. But in spite of the warning, his kiss quickly began to heat her blood and send her arms wrapping tightly around his neck. After that, her resistance walked right out the door and into the cold night.

When the need for air finally pulled their lips apart, she spoke in an urgent rush. "You're not playing fair, Russ. I can't make sense of anything like this."

Rising to his feet, he pulled her along with him, then before she could guess his intentions, he bent down and swept her into the cradle of his arms.

With his lips brushing against her ear, he whispered, "I never planned on playing fair. Not about getting you into my arms. We'll make sense later. Right now I'm going to show you my bed and exactly why you belong there—with me."

As Russ carried her through the house, she realized that on so many levels she was a coward. But she was also a woman with a woman's needs. And tonight she couldn't deny herself the pleasure of being loved by this man.

Later, she promised herself, after the hunger in her heart had eased and the fire in her loins had burned itself out, she'd find the courage to tell him that she could never be his wife.

Chapter Ten

Much later that night, Laurel rolled away from Russ's arms and sat up on the edge of the bed.

"It's getting very late, Russ. And I can see through the window that it's snowing again. If I wait around much longer, I'll slip and slide all the way down the hill."

Groaning, he caught her by the arm and pulled her back down on the mattress. "Why do you need to get down the hill? My truck is a four-wheel drive. We'll go to work together—from here."

"I'm not going to spend the night with you," she countered, even as he tucked her back beneath the covers.

His warm, naked body felt wonderful against hers, and no doubt it would be heavenly to let herself fall asleep in his arms. But she didn't want him to get the impression that she was changing her mind and giving in to his wishes.

"Is there something at your place that's better than this?" he murmured as he nuzzled his nose against the side of her neck.

All Laurel wanted to do was turn and press the front of her body next to his, to invite him to make love to her all over again. She'd thought that after a few hours, her desire for him would die down; instead it was like a low, steady flame, just waiting for him to fuel it to a torrid fire.

"I didn't come up here to fall in bed with you," she pointed out. "I came up here to talk. And so far I've not said what I need to say."

Ignoring her neck, he pressed soft kisses over her cheek. The sweet sensation sent goose bumps rushing up and down her arms. "Okay, I'm listening," he murmured. "I'm ready to hear you say yes to my marriage proposal."

"You call what you did this morning a proposal?" she asked in dismay. "That was more like a boss giving an order."

He stroked his fingers through her long hair. "I'm sorry, Laurel. A cow pasture isn't the place for a man to propose to his sweetheart, but I couldn't hold back my feelings—it all just came out before I could stop it." His arm curved over her waist as he urged her closer. "I'll make it up to you, baby. I promise I can be romantic if you'll give me the chance."

A soft sigh of regret passed her lips. She'd never had much romance in her life, but that was of little consequence now. "Whether you proposed in a cow pasture or on some moonlit beach doesn't matter," she murmured.

"My answer would still be no. I meant what I said this morning, Russ. It's an affair or nothing at all."

Something in her voice must have sounded convincing, because he sat up in bed and stared down at her face. "An affair!" he practically spat. "You're not that type, Laurel. Don't try to pretend that you are."

"I'm here in your bed, aren't I?" she asked in a calm, reasonable voice. "That should be proof enough that I'm not waiting for marriage."

Reaching across her, he switched on a lamp resting on the nightstand. As he sat up, the circle of light illuminated his face and Laurel could see he was incensed. His jaw was tight, his lips clamped to a thin line.

"Why are you doing this to me? To yourself? We just made love, Laurel. And don't try to tell me it was just sex. I know when a woman is having 'just sex.' Brooke taught me that much! And that's not what I felt with you."

Looking away from him, she shut her eyes tightly. "Okay, Russ, I do feel something for you and maybe it is love. But love doesn't fix everything." Opening her eyes, she twisted her head back around so that she could look up at him. "If I had years to try to explain, I doubt that would be enough time. Because—well, I can't explain how I feel."

The tension on his face suddenly eased and he gently rubbed his hand up and down her arm. "Maybe you should try."

Feeling as though a dead weight had fallen to the pit of her stomach, Laurel scooted off the bed and began to gather up her clothing. "Look, Russ, I've told you enough about my family life for you to see that it wasn't pretty. My dad was never really one of those stand-up guys who took care of things and met his responsibilities as a husband or father. Oh, he worked and paid the bills, but other than that it was my mom who kept the family emotionally connected. When she left—I was so young, and my sister desperately needed someone to care for her and reassure her. I had to be that someone."

She stepped into her skirt, then zipped it closed at the back. While she tugged her top over her head, Russ asked, "What about your brother? Surely he cared about his sisters."

Snorting with disgust, she wrapped the belt around her waist. "Garth was just like Dad. There, but always detached and living in his own little world. After Mom left, I honestly don't think either of them knew what to do." She buckled the belt, then paused to look at him. "I guess what I'm trying to say is—I never got to be a child, so how could I possibly know how to raise one. I don't even want to try!"

"Why? Because you're afraid if you have a child it might die? Like your sister died?"

His questions were like a knife blade sinking into the middle of her chest. Pain radiated up her throat and down both arms, and when she spoke, her voice was little more than a hoarse whisper.

"Maybe. That's part of it. And maybe I poured so much caretaking and love into Lainey that there just isn't anything left in me to give to a child of my own."

He scooted off the bed, and Laurel felt sick and weak as his hand closed around her upper arm. She realized she must sound very bitter and selfish, and even more, cowardly. But it was better that he understood her feelings now rather than later.

"Tell that to someone else, Laurel. Because I sure as hell don't believe it. For five years I've seen you nurse and nurture and love every animal we came in contact with, even the mean ones that lashed out at you. You have plenty of love to give to me and the children we could have. You're just too afraid to try."

Feeling as though she could hardly argue that point, she turned her back to him. "And why shouldn't I be afraid?" she muttered. "Lainey died of a blood disease, and me being her twin makes it a possibility that I could develop it, too!"

The grip on her arm eased. "Is that what doctors have told you? That you have a high risk of getting the same thing?"

"No. None of them call it a high risk. But on the other hand, none of the doctors I've talked to can completely assure me that I'll remain free of the disease." She whirled back around to him. "Don't you see, Russ? I'm risky business. It wouldn't be fair to you, or any man for that matter, to put such uncertainty in your life. And it certainly wouldn't be good for a child. God knows, I understand what it's like to lose my mother. And so do you. I can't bear to think of putting a child through that sort of torture."

Nuzzling his face against the side of her hair, he said gently, "Oh, Laurel, Laurel. I can appreciate your fears. But as far as I'm concerned, you don't have a good argument. Okay, so you haven't had a perfect childhood. And it's likely that health issues do run in your family genes. You're just one of millions facing the same sort of problems."

Easing slightly back, she stared at him in stunned wonder. "How could you be so dismissive, so casual about it all? You can't understand! If you did you wouldn't—"

A mixture of anger and disgust tightened his features. "Don't start that with me, Laurel! Don't act like you're the only human being that's ever dealt with a broken home life or the loss of a loved one. What the hell do you think I've gone through, a picnic? I know all about watching a loved one die and feeling totally lost and helpless. And I've gone through my share of loving and losing and betrayal. But that doesn't mean I'm going to lie down and give up."

She jerked her arm away from his grip. "You have to be the most—insensitive man that's walked this earth!"

"Why? Because I won't coddle you, stroke the top of your head and say poor, poor Laurel, your life was over before it could ever get started? If you're expecting that from me, then you've got me confused with someone else."

"No! I don't want your sympathy. In fact, I don't want anything from you."

Fighting the urge to cry, she found her boots and tugged them on. A few steps away, Russ jerked on his jeans and shirt.

"Well, let me tell you something, Laurel. If all you want from me is an affair, then forget it. I happen to believe I'm better than that. I happen to believe I deserve a woman who wants to love me and be my wife. One who would gladly bear my children. I won't settle for less."

It was all Laurel could do to keep from breaking into sobs, but as she turned to face him, she swallowed them down and squared her shoulders. "Aren't you expecting too much too soon from me? We've only just now become lovers. Now you're wanting to leap into marriage and babies. Why?"

"Why not?" he shot back at her. "It's not like we're strangers, Laurel. My Lord, we've been practically side by side for the past five years and gone through everything imaginable together. We might not have been aware of each other's past family history, but we know what kind of people we are now. And most of all, we love each other. We belong together. And not as just two people who sometimes sleep together, but as man and wife."

She was suddenly trembling. "Do we? Then why did it take you five years to realize it?"

Closing the short space between them, he wrapped his big hands around her shoulders. "Okay, Laurel, I'm guilty of having my head stuck in the sand. Or maybe I should say stuck in my work. That night I kissed you for the first time, I went home thinking what a blind idiot I'd been. And then I started thinking about all the time that I've wasted—all the time that we could have been together."

His admission left her far more thoughtful than angry, and she studied his face as her mind whirled for answers. "You got all of that from one kiss? Come on, Russ. I'm inexperienced, but I'm not that naive."

A grimace tightened his lips. "Okay. Maybe it was more than just the kiss that got me thinking."

Dropping his hands from her shoulders, he moved away from her and over to the window. As he pushed the curtain aside, Laurel could see the night sky was nearly white with snowfall. The sight left her chilled, but not nearly as cold as leaving Russ's arms.

"Like what?"

When he didn't answer immediately, Laurel strode over to where he stood. He looked away from the window and around to her.

"Several things all rolled together," he said.

His evasive answer caused her jaw to tighten with frustration. "Do you want to know what I was thinking whenever you told me about this job change? I wasn't thinking you needed to ease your hours or get away from the public demand. I thought it had something to do with a woman."

Turning away from the window, he studied her for long moments and then he said, "In a way you're right. It was a woman. And the woman wasn't you. Not at first."

Laurel felt as though he'd struck her. "What does that mean?" she asked, then swiftly shook her head. "Never mind. I don't think I want to hear this."

She turned away from him, but his hand caught her arm and urged her back.

"I wasn't going to say anything about this. Because I wasn't sure how you'd take it, or if you'd even understand. But now I see that I need to tell you."

Staring at him, she waited for him to continue.

"A couple of months ago—just before Christmas, I'd stopped by the Blue Mesa for lunch. While I was there I spotted Brooke—eating with some friends of hers."

"Your ex-wife? She was back in Ruidoso?"

He nodded. "As you might guess, it was a shock to see her."

Laurel felt as though the breath was being squeezed from her lungs. "Did you speak to her?"

"I didn't plan to. But she happened to see me as she passed my table. We exchanged hellos and she asked me how I was doing." The corners of his mouth turned downward. "I didn't have to ask how her life had been going. She appeared to be at least seven or eight months pregnant."

Laurel gasped. "Pregnant! But you told me she didn't want to have children."

"She didn't. Not with me." His head swung back and forth. "Seeing her like that opened my eyes, Laurel. In ways you can't imagine."

Unconsciously, she pressed a hand to the ache in the middle of her chest. "Why? Because you wished she was still your wife? That it was your baby she was carrying?"

"No! Hell no."

Dazed, she turned and walked back over to the bed. Sinking weakly onto the edge, she shook her head. "Oh God, Russ, do you know how all of this sounds? Like you saw your ex-wife and realized you had to settle for me. Well, I might seem easy to you, but I'm not a substitute!"

Rushing over to her, he tugged her to her feet. "Laurel, that's not what any of this means! Seeing her made me recognize all the mistakes I'd made in the past. Even worse, the mistakes I was still making. That's when I decided I had to change things. My job—my life. And then when you said you might not come here to the ranch with me, I realized just how lost I'd be without you."

"How convenient for you that I was willing to tag along," she said, her voice flat and empty. "That I fell into your bed like a pathetic spinster."

"Laurel, you haven't listened to a thing I've said!"

"Excuse me, Russ, but I've listened to all I'm going to." Pulling away from him, she hurried from the bedroom. Out in the living room, she snatched her coat from the closet and was tugging it on when he walked into the room.

"What are you going to do, Laurel? Run from me? From everything that scares you?"

"You don't want me, Russ. You want a wife and a baby." With the hood of her coat fastened tightly beneath her chin, she strode purposely toward the front door. Russ followed close on her heels.

"And what do you want, Laurel?" He flung the question at her. "Maybe you should think about that long and hard."

Not bothering to answer, she jerked open the door and stepped out into the snowy night.

Normally Laurel was quite comfortable with the cold weather here in the mountains of Lincoln County. But this evening the confrontation with Russ had sucked every bit of warmth from her body. By the time she got to her house, she was literally shivering.

Inside, she quickly turned up the thermostat, then after shedding her coat, hurried to the fireplace to build a fire. As she stacked the paper and kindling, she tried not to think about the night Russ had shown her how to start the flames and keep them going. She didn't want to remember how special that evening had been, when they'd made love for the very first time.

And ever since that night, she'd been agonizing over the fact that she wasn't good enough to be Russ's wife. That she didn't have the right background or a strong enough constitution to be the woman who could make him happy. But now she could see those things were the least of her problems. He'd seen his pregnant ex-wife and had suddenly decided he wanted a family for himself. Laurel just happened to be the nearest female for him to latch onto.

So what are you crying about, Laurel? You've been telling him and yourself that you didn't want him to love you. That you wanted to keep your relationship casual. Now you're feeling betrayed. You need to get a grip!

Russ was right about one thing, she thought, as she stuck a burning match to the kindling. She needed to decide what she really wanted in her life. A family with him or a safe, solitary existence.

Chapter Eleven

The next morning, several inches of snow was on the ground, and as seemed to happen with storms and weather changes, animals chose that time to give birth. As a result, three of the young heifers that had been prematurely bred needed assistance in calving. Thankfully, none of them needed cesareans, but all three births were difficult, requiring Russ and Laurel to do lots of physical pulling.

Between the birthing and tending the sick, quarantined cattle, Russ had very little opportunity to ponder on all that had happened between him and Laurel last night. Not that thinking would help matters, he thought grimly. He'd already spent most of last night trying to stop his mind from spinning with thoughts about the woman, and he still couldn't quit trying to make sense of her reaction.

She'd misconstrued the whole thing about Brooke,

but, damn it, Russ wasn't going to start having regrets about telling her. He wanted everything between him and Laurel to be open and honest. After having a wife who'd deceived and hidden the truth from him, he wouldn't settle for anything less.

"How are they doing, Russ? Think they're going to make it?"

At the sound of Maccoy's voice, Russ turned away from the cow to see the older man standing just outside the pen, leaning against a fence post.

Russ ambled tiredly over to the man he'd worked with for the past twelve years. He supposed Maccoy was the closest thing he'd ever had to a father, and that included the uncle he'd lived with after his mother's death.

"Better today. Even the sickest ones are getting better, but it's going to take some time before they'll be well enough to turn back out to pasture."

"Well, at least they're going to make it," Maccoy remarked. "I'm not sure I can say the same for you, though. You look like hell."

Russ swiped a weary hand over his face. "It's been a long day, that's all."

"Yeah, you've been damned busy since you got here to the ranch. Are you regrettin' the move?"

Off to their left, he could see Laurel walking down the alleyway of the barn, toward their office. This morning when he'd arrived to work, she was already here, drinking coffee with Maccoy. She'd greeted him warmly enough, and throughout the day she'd followed his orders to the letter, without one complaint or disagreement. But even when she'd been working close at his side, her coolness had been so tangible he'd expected ice to form on her clothing.

"No. Are you?"

"Hell no! This is a breeze for me. Didn't even have to scrape the snow off my truck this morning. Just walked over from the bunkhouse."

He grinned tiredly at the older man, then called out to Laurel before she got too far away to hear him.

Turning abruptly on her heel, she walked back to where the two men stood at the small cattle pen. Sidling up to Maccoy, she darted a glance at Russ before purposely setting her gaze on the penned cattle.

"You need something?" she asked.

Yes, I need for you to be reasonable, to realize how much we need to be together. But even if he did dare to speak those words in front of Maccoy, they wouldn't make an impact on her. No, he was going to have to come up with something more than talk to make her see they belonged together.

"Yes," he said aloud. "I want you to change the water in this trough and add more electrolytes. Enough to treat each cow at eight hundred pounds weight volume. And don't let them drink until you get it thoroughly mixed. You might need to get one of the cowboys to help you."

Maccoy frowned at him. "What's the matter with you helping her?"

It wasn't like the older man to question Russ's orders, and he wondered if Maccoy had already guessed that something more personal was going on between him and Laurel.

"Laramie and the hands just brought in another heifer that's close to calving. She's penned outside the barn. I've got to go deal with her."

"Damn, must be a full moon," Maccoy remarked. "All the females around here are getting stirred up."

"You can say that again," Russ muttered.

From the corner of his eye, he watched Laurel cut

a sharp gaze in his direction. "Yeah, blame it on the moon," she said dryly. "For your information, it's in the first quarter. That's how much you men know about it."

Russ let himself out of the pen and paused near her shoulder. "Maybe I should have studied the calendar last night and I might have been prepared."

She turned and stalked off. His jaw tight, Russ watched her go. "I'll be outside with the heifer," he said to Maccoy, then moved away from the pen.

In spite of his bowed back and gimpy leg, Maccoy somehow managed to keep up with Russ's long stride as the two men made their way toward the barn exit.

"What's up with you and Laurel? She don't act too happy."

"That's because she isn't," Russ snapped.

"Oh." After they'd traveled several steps, Maccoy added, "Well, I got the impression she liked it here on the Chaparral."

"She does. She—well, I've been pushing her."

"Pushing her? Hell, Russ, you pushed her way harder at the clinic. She's on a picnic here."

Russ stifled a groan. There was no point in keeping secrets from the old man. Especially when he was close to both Laurel and Russ. "I'm not talking about work now, Maccoy. I—" He stopped his forward movement and turned to look at Maccoy, who'd halted alongside him. "I might as well tell you—I asked Laurel to marry me. And she's all upset about the whole thing."

A wide grin suddenly split across the older man's face. "Now, that's some good news! And about time, too, if you ask me."

"Hell, Maccoy, didn't you hear me? She gave me a big, loud no. She's… Well, she doesn't want to be my wife."

"That's why she's angry? 'Cause you proposed to her? That don't make sense, Russ. She could've said no without getting mad about it." Shaking his head, he reached over and patted Russ's shoulder. "Forget all that nonsense. She'll say yes—eventually. I'll bet on it."

Russ grimaced. "I wouldn't put too much money on the wager, Maccoy. You need to remember I don't exactly have a good track record with women."

"Bah. What the hell did Brooke know? The woman was no good from the start. But Laurel. She's a keeper. A real keeper."

Releasing a weary breath, Russ said, "I wished you'd let me in on that sooner. Seems like I'm always slow about waking up and seeing what's right in front of me. I wasted time in getting rid of Brooke, and now I've messed up by not courting Laurel years ago."

The older man gave Russ's shoulder another comforting pat. "You'll figure things out with Laurel. Just let her know you love her. 'Cause I don't think that girl has had much of that in her life. People like her—sometimes it's hard for them to accept love."

He cast a sly look at Maccoy. "Where did you learn so much about such things?"

"I may not look like it now, but I once turned a few female heads. Mae was going to marry me, too, but then she had to get sick and die on me. I shouldn't have dallied around about asking her. At least I would've had a wife for a while."

"Well, you might have got your timing wrong with Mae. But you're damned right about Laurel not having much love in her life. And that's something I'm going to do my best to change," Russ told him, then hurried out of the barn to tend the waiting heifer.

* * *

Two busy weeks had passed when Laurel got the news that Alexa and her two children had arrived on the ranch. Hardly able to contain her excitement, she informed Maccoy where she'd be and practically raced across the ranch yard to the big two-story house.

As soon as she entered the atrium, she could hear childish shrieks in the kitchen. When she stepped inside, she could see where the sound was coming from. A little boy that looked very much like Alexa's husband, Jonas, was riding a stick horse at a reckless gallop through the kitchen.

"Jonas David! That's enough or I'm going to take Silver away from you and tie him in the broom closet!" Alexa warned the boy.

Giggling mischievously, he stopped long enough to give his mother a daring grin. "Silver wouldn't like it there! I'm gonna take him outside," the boy exclaimed, then as he darted toward the door, he spotted Laurel and jammed on the brakes, which in this case was a pair of brown cowboy boots.

"Who are you?" he asked curiously.

Bending down to the boy's level, she said in a gentle voice, "I'm Laurel. And you must be Jonas."

She'd not seen Alexa's first child since her friend had given birth to him here at the Chaparral nearly four years ago. He'd grown into an adorable boy with thick brown hair and freckled nose. His blue eyes sparkled with high spirits, and Laurel was surprised at how much she wanted to gather him up in her arms and squish him with affection.

The child nodded just as Alexa spotted her and squealed with joy.

"Laurel!" She practically ran across the room, and

Laurel felt her eyes mist over as the other woman hugged her tightly. "We didn't hear you come in, did we, Reena?"

The cook laughed. "How could we with little Jonas turning the kitchen into a racetrack."

Grabbing her by the hand, Alexa pulled her over to the middle of the kitchen, where Reena was standing at the work island peeling a pile of turnips.

"Look at her, Reena! Isn't she lovely," Alexa exclaimed.

Laurel rolled her eyes at her friend's description. "Oh, sure. I always look my best with cow manure on my boots and jeans and my hair looking like I had a fight with a bear."

"Laurel always looks lovely," Reena answered Alexa's question. "Especially when she smiles. But here lately I haven't seen very much smiling from her."

Laurel shrugged out of her coat, and Alexa peered anxiously at her as she took the garment from her and hung it on the back of a nearby chair.

"Please don't tell me you're unhappy here," her friend pleaded. "Quint has already been telling me what a great asset you and Russ are to the ranch. We're so glad to have you both."

"The ranch is wonderful," Laurel assured her. "And beautiful. I can see why you love it."

Smiling, Alexa slung her arm around Laurel's shoulders. "I hope you're beginning to love it, too."

By now little Jonas had kicked his stick pony back into a trot. As Laurel watched the boy, she was reminded all over again of Russ's revelation of Brooke's pregnancy. She wasn't sure why his confession had left her so tortured. It wasn't as if the woman was actually having Russ's child. But something about the thought of his ex-wife pushing him to propose marriage to Laurel hadn't set well. It still didn't sit well. But she was trying her best to forget it and him.

"I can't believe your son has grown up so," Laurel said, and this time she gave her friend a genuine smile. "He's so adorable. And where is your daughter?"

"Upstairs, taking a nap. Or, she was the last time I looked. Sassy is keeping an eye on her for me. Would you like to go peek at her?" Alexa invited.

"I really should be getting back to work," Laurel said as she glanced briefly at her watch. "But I'll go take a short peek. I want to see if she really looks as much like you as she does in the photos you sent me."

"Great!" She latched onto Laurel's hand and started out of the kitchen. "Reena, would you—"

"Yes, I'll keep an eye on the little man while you two are gone," the cook finished before Alexa could ask the question.

"Thanks, Reena!"

Outside the kitchen they walked down a short hallway until they reached an open doorway. Beyond that was the stairs leading up to the second story. As the two women made the long climb, Alexa kept Laurel's hand firmly ensconced in hers. The physical connection took her back to their school days, when they'd laughed and giggled and revealed their innermost secrets to each other.

"It's great to have you here, Alexa. You can't imagine how much I miss you being around."

The lovely, black-haired woman shot Laurel a tender smile. "And I miss seeing you. One of these days, when Jonas retires from the Rangers, we'll get to spend more time here. And that's something I'm very much looking forward to."

"When is he planning that?" Laurel asked.

"Well, he's been a Texas Ranger for nearly fourteen years. I expect he'll go to twenty or more. It's something he loves and I'm very proud of him, as you might guess."

"He didn't come with you this time?"

Alexa shook her head. "This coming week he has to testify in court over in Harris County—that's in Houston. Since he has to be away for several days, he thought it might be a good opportunity for me and the kids to come out here for a visit. I wish he could have come, too. But hopefully he can next time."

By now the two of them had reached the landing, and Alexa led her to an open door to one of the many bedrooms.

"I'll be very quiet so as not to wake her," Laurel whispered as they entered the room.

Alexa chuckled. "Believe me, you don't have to whisper. She sleeps through anything. Since Jonas David was still fairly little when I gave birth to her, I guess she naturally got used to his loud bawling. Mother says he was the worst squall bag she'd ever seen."

At the side of the bed, Laurel stared down at the little girl curled up on the wide mattress. Her hair was as black as her mother's and hung in soft tendrils around her cherubic face. It wasn't often that Laurel was around children. Now as she studied this one, a painful longing struck her, and suddenly she desperately wanted to know how it would feel to hold a child of her own, to feel its warmth and to know that life came from her and the man she loved. Oh, God, how wonderful that would be. But if something went wrong, as it had with Lainey, what would she do? How would she cope?

"Her skin looks like she's come right out of an English rose garden," Laurel said with hushed awe. "It's so smooth and creamy. She doesn't have one freckle like her brother. She's a beautiful child, Alexa."

"Jonas says he wishes she wasn't so pretty," Alexa said with a wry smile. "He doesn't want her to get married until she's thirty."

Turning away from the bed, Laurel started out of the bedroom and Alexa followed.

"You say thirty like that would make Jessica an old maid. I'm thirty, Alexa."

The other woman groaned. "Laurel, don't be so sensitive. I didn't mean anything like that." As the two women stepped out of the room and onto the landing, she wrapped her arm affectionately through Laurel's. "But now that you've brought up the subject, you are getting on in years."

Realizing her friend was teasing, Laurel tried to laugh, but it came out more like a strangled sob. "Oh, Alexa—so much has happened since I moved out here to the ranch. And now—"

The agony in Laurel's voice instantly wiped the smile from Alexa's face. "Laurel, honey, what in the world? If something isn't right, you should have already told me! All you had to do was pick up the phone and punch my number."

"It's not the job. It's—" Laurel broke off with a shake of her head. "I don't have time for this now. I've got to get back to the barn."

"Not hardly! If a vet and twenty-five or more cowhands can't take care of things for thirty minutes without you, then this place is falling apart." She pulled on Laurel's arm. "Let's go to my room where we can talk in private."

When they entered the bedroom, Laurel was amazed to see it was furnished basically as it had been when

Alexa was still living at home. And though her surroundings should have been inconsequential at the moment, Laurel was struck by them. Some good things never changed, she thought. At least not for other people. Laurel would never have a home where she could go to find her family, to find that her memory was still cherished and loved.

After closing the door behind them, Alexa sat Laurel down in a big, overstuffed armchair and then took a seat for herself on the end of the bed.

"Okay, we're alone. Now, tell me everything. And I won't let you out of here until you do," she warned. "What's happened?"

Laurel scrubbed her face with both hands, then let out a long sigh. "Russ asked me to marry him. That's what!"

Alexa's eyes grew wide and then with a loud joyful squeal, she leaped off the bed and clasped Laurel's face between her hands. "Oh, honey, this is wonderful news. I'm so happy for you. So happy!"

By the time she smacked kisses on Laurel's cheeks, tears were filling her eyes.

"Alexa—wait! You're getting way ahead of yourself. I told him no."

Jerking upright, her friend planted her hands on her hips as she stared at Laurel in disbelief. "What? Are you kidding me?"

"Do you honestly think I would joke about something like that?"

Alexa rolled her eyes. "Right. I should know better—Laurel Stanton doesn't know how to joke." She stabbed Laurel with an annoyed look. "So why, pray tell me, did you say no?"

Unable to stay seated, Laurel jumped to her feet. "I

shouldn't have to tell you the reasons. You know my problems!"

"Reasons! Problems! Oh, God, Laurel—you make me so angry."

Her nostrils flaring, she moved away from Alexa and began to wander aimlessly around the room. "I make Russ angry, too. In fact, we're hardly speaking at the moment. I mean, at work we communicate as we need to. But anything more is—"

Bending her head, she swallowed hard as tears threatened to overtake her. After a few moments passed, she felt Alexa's hand on her shoulder.

"Laurel, honey," she said softly, "I'm sorry if I've upset you. But I meant to. Something or someone needs to shake you and make you see how you're punishing yourself for no good reason."

Lifting her head, she looked through a wall of tears at the closest and dearest friend she'd ever had. "Punishing myself? Is that what you think I'm doing? I'm trying to be sensible. I don't have the background to be a wife. And I especially don't have what it takes to be a mother!"

"Really? How does anyone know for sure unless they try?"

"And what if I did try and failed? Russ doesn't deserve that! He's already had one worthless wife, and I've seen with my own eyes how long it's taken him to get over divorcing her. In fact, I'm not quite sure he is over it," she muttered.

"What does that mean?" Alexa prodded.

Grimacing, Laurel looked away from her and released a heavy sigh. "He confessed that he saw her back in December at the Blue Mesa. He said they did little more than exchange hellos, and I believe him about that. But he admitted that seeing her had shaken him. In fact, it shook him so much that he decided to change his job. See, Brooke was very pregnant, and that—she—made him realize it was time he took another wife and started a family."

"Is there anything really so strange in that?" Alexa asked gently. "Sometimes seeing someone from your past puts a person to thinking, especially about the choices we make in our lives. Besides, I don't really think you're worried about Russ's feelings for Brooke. Are you?"

With a rueful shake of her head, Laurel said, "Not really. When he first told me about it, I was a bit angry and hurt. But then I realized I had no right to be. He's not my husband."

"But he wants to be your husband. My word, Laurel, you should be jumping for joy! You've loved the man for a long, long time."

Laurel's mouth fell open. "I—I've never said that to you! I didn't even mention my feelings for Russ until a few weeks ago when we talked about me moving out here to the ranch. And I haven't loved him for a long, long time. I'm not even sure that I love him now!"

A shrewd smile spread across Alexa's face. "You can't fool me, any more than you can fool yourself."

Turning away from her friend, Laurel began to pace around the spacious bedroom. "Listen, Alexa, I tried to tell Russ that I wasn't up to marriage and kids. I told him that all I wanted was an affair and—"

"An affair!" Alexa interrupted with dismay. "That's terrible."

Stopping in her tracks, Laurel challenged, "Why is it? People do it all the time. Russ and I could enjoy each other's company and not have all the heartbreak that goes with marriage and kids."

"Ha! You think not having a piece of paper between you is going to keep everything safe and neat?"

"It doesn't matter," Laurel answered glumly. "He won't go for that idea anyway."

"I don't blame the man. If you don't want to give him everything, then he needs to tell you to get lost!"

"You should be happy, because he's pretty much told me that already."

Seeing the misery on Laurel's face, Alexa relented and with a commiserating expression, walked over to her.

"Laurel, I'm sorry if I'm hurting you. But what I've been saying shouldn't surprise you. I want the same happiness for you that I have with Jonas and the children. And I believe that deep down you want that same thing, too."

Laurel's eyes welled with tears as she released a long sigh of resignation. "Of course, I want it. But not everyone can have what they want, Alexa. What if I became ill like Lainey? What if—"

"What if I was in a fatal car accident? What if I developed a disease or, God forbid, one of my children did? Life is full of what-ifs, Laurel! Don't waste yours by trying to dodge all the obstacles that are thrown at you. Instead, be fearless and jump straight over them."

"That takes courage. And I'm not sure I have it."

Leaning forward, Alexa pressed an encouraging kiss to Laurel's cheek. "I'm certain that you do."

"I'll think about it. Now I'd better get back to the barn." She started out of the bedroom and Alexa followed.

"Okay. I'll see you tomorrow night—if not before," she said.

Puzzled by that remark, Laurel paused on the landing. "What's tomorrow night?"

"Dinner. Quint and his family and Grandfather Abe are all coming. We want you and Russ and Maccoy to attend, too. So wear something pretty," she added impishly.

For Russ's sake? Did Laurel really want to attract his attention in that way? She couldn't deny that she did. No more than she could deny to herself that she'd missed being physically close to him these past two weeks. She'd missed seeing warmth in his eyes and hearing his voice gentle with tenderness whenever he spoke to her.

"I'll try to be presentable," she promised, then turned and hurried down the stairs.

She was out of the house and halfway to the barn when her cell rang. Seeing the caller was Russ, she answered it promptly.

"Come down to the calving area," he said without preamble. "I need you."

"I'm on my way."

Five minutes later, she found him in one of the birthing stalls with a cow that had just given birth to twins. The sight of the identical babies lying on the straw, their black hair still damp with birthing fluid, drew a squeal of delight from Laurel.

"Oh, my! They're beautiful!" Forgetting the cool wall that had been standing between them for days, she grinned at Russ, then quickly sank to her knees near the babies. "Are they okay?"

"They check out fine. And you can see for yourself that the mother is already up and ready to nurse them. That's where you come in."

"Me? But if she's fine—"

"She's fine," he interrupted. "But she won't have enough milk for both of them. I want the smaller one on the mother. The larger one will have to be bottle fed. I could have Laramie give the job to one of the cowboys, but I thought you might want to do it."

Laurel turned a pleading gaze on him. "Oh, Russ, are you sure it has to be this way? It will be awful to tear the twins apart. And the bigger one needs her mother just as much as the smaller one does."

For the first time in days, the angles of his face softened with understanding. "I'm sorry, Laurel. I wish we could keep them all together, too. But both calves deserve the best of care. And we don't want to compromise the mother's health, either."

Laurel looked back at the twins. Both calves were attempting to rise to their knees, but were still a bit too wobbly to make it all the way up on all fours. "They're girls," Laurel said, her voice dropping to a ragged whisper. "Sisters shouldn't have to be separated, Russ. Let me bottle feed both of them. Please!"

Suddenly he squatted down beside her, and as his hand settled warmly on her shoulder, Laurel closed her eyes against an onslaught of emotions.

"Laurel, you've worked with me for a long time—you know I wouldn't be doing this unless it was absolutely necessary. The small one has a much better chance to survive on its mother's nutrients. Sometimes it just has to be this way. Can you handle this job? I'll understand if you can't."

Opening her eyes, she turned her head to look at him and the gentleness in his brown gaze made her heart beat with heavy regret.

*Don't waste your life trying to avoid all the obstacles
thrown at you. Be fearless and jump straight over them.*

Oh, God, she prayed. Why couldn't she find the courage to reach for everything she wanted? Why couldn't
she meet her fears head-on?

Blinking at the moisture in her eyes, she said, "I
can do it."

"Good." He touched his fingertips to her cheek. "And
by the way, I've missed you, Laurel."

Pain spread through the middle of her chest. "I've
not gone anywhere," she pointed out.

"Oh, yes you have. You've gone far, far away from
me," he murmured. "When are you going to come
back?"

Everything inside her was aching to throw her arms
around his neck and bury her face against his neck. But
common sense told her that once she touched him, she'd
be lost. And she couldn't allow that to happen. No matter how much she wanted it.

"Russ—I—why can't you forget? That's what we
both need to do."

His hand gently cupped her jaw. "I can't do that, Laurel. Not any more than you can."

The temptation to give in to him was so intense it
frightened her, and in an effort to put some space between them, she quickly jumped to her feet.

"We need to— I have to—"

"Hey, Russ."

The ranch hand's voice cut through Laurel's tangled
words and she looked around with relief to see Guy, a
tall, young cowboy with dark hair and a bright yellow
bandanna tied around his neck, approaching the stall.

Russ straightened to his full height. "What is it,
Guy?"

"Sorry for interrupting, doc. Guess this is turning out to be a busy day. We need you over in the foaling barn. Laramie's best cutting mare is having some trouble."

"Tell him I'll be right there," Russ instructed.

The cowboy turned on his heel and hurried away. Ross glanced regretfully at Laurel.

She quickly turned to business. "I'll go find a place to put the calf. And don't worry, I'll take the best care of her."

"I never worry about your care of an animal, Laurel. But you and me—we can't go on like this."

"You're right. We can't."

His gaze searched her face for long moments and Laurel was beginning to think he was going to say more on the subject, but he gave his head a rueful shake and muttered, "I gotta go."

Laurel watched him leave the stall before she turned back to the tiny twins. While she and Russ had been talking, the bigger calf had managed to get to her feet and wobble over to the mother.

As Laurel watched the baby search for the comfort of her mother's milk, tears streamed down her face.

How was she going to take this precious baby away from its mother and sister? The same way she was going to end her relationship with Russ. By convincing herself it was the only way they could all survive.

Sniffing back her tears, she walked over and gathered the calf in her arms.

"Come on, baby girl. It's going to be just you and me now."

Chapter Twelve

Russ had never been a fan of dinner parties. During his marriage to Brooke, he'd been forced to attend events that were all about money and social appearances, neither of which he cared about. But he'd escorted his wife because he'd wanted to support her so-called climb up the corporate ladder.

But that unfortunate part of his life was over, and tonight was different. Tonight he was among friends and folks with the same interests he held. And Laurel would be attending. That had been reason enough for him to pull on a white shirt with his blue jeans and tighten a bolo tie around his neck.

Now as he shared a cocktail with Laramie, Maccoy and the Cantrell men, Russ found himself watching the doorway leading into the family room and wondering when she was finally going to appear.

For the past two and a half weeks, he'd had to fight

with himself to keep from saying to hell with it all. If she wanted an affair, he'd give her one. That would be better than having nothing between them but a wall of frost. But what he wanted from Laurel was far more than physical. And if he gave in to her now, he might never win her over to the idea of marriage.

When Laurel did finally appear, Russ found himself practically gawking at her like a teenager. She was wearing a deep purple dress of some clingy sort of fabric that accentuated her curves and stopped just above her knees. A pair of black strappy high heels gave her legs a sleek, dancer's look, making it impossible to keep his gaze from sliding up and down the smooth arc of her calves.

Russ hadn't even known the woman owned such shoes, much less a dress that looked so downright sexy. Her hair was pinned atop her head in graceful loops and emerald-colored earrings sparkled at her earlobes. If she was trying to make him cave to her way of thinking, she was damned near to succeeding, he thought helplessly.

For the next few minutes, while everyone chatted and finished their drinks, Laurel remained on the opposite side of the room, where she'd taken a seat next to Alexa and Abe, the eighty-five-year-old patriarch of the Cantrell family. But once dinner was announced and everyone filed into the dining room, Russ was pleasantly surprised to discover that Laurel had been seated by him.

Once they were settled in their chairs, he tilted his head toward hers and spoke in a voice for her ears only. "Looks like someone decided we should be together."

Darting him a glance, she said, "I'm sure it was Alexa. She happens to believe we make a perfect pair."

"Smart woman. And beautiful, too. Almost as beautiful as you."

She turned her head and with her brows arched, she looked straight at him. "I clean up well, but I can't compare to Alexa."

"When you stop underselling yourself, Laurel, then you're going to realize that the two of us do belong together."

He could see an array of conflicting emotions flicker in her eyes, but what, if any, remark she might have said was suddenly interrupted as Abe asked the guests to lower their heads while he prayed a blessing over the meal.

For the next hour, Russ kept any personal remarks he had for Laurel to himself. Instead, he joined in the general discussion around the table about the ranching business and what the coming spring was going to hold in store for the Chaparral. Laramie was never much of a talker, but Quint and Abe made up for any slack in the conversation. Russ wasn't surprised to see that Alexa, and Quint's wife, Maura, were both highly informed on the subject of raising cattle and horses. Both women had come from ranching families. What did surprise him tonight, however, was the fact that Reena was sitting at the table as a guest, rather than simply working as the cook. Not only that, she was seated at Abe's side and the older man had been casting plenty of flirtatious looks at her.

Maybe by the time Russ reached Abe's age, he'd be an expert on how to handle a stubborn woman like Laurel, he thought wistfully. But he doubted it. Age had nothing to do with love. It knew no age or color, or boundary. It either existed or it didn't. And he desperately hoped that whatever was in Laurel's heart would take root and grow until it was too big for her to ignore.

Long after the meal was over, Russ was in the family room, about to say good-night to his friends, when Alexa came up to him and pulled him away from the group of men.

"Sorry to interrupt," she spoke in a low voice, "but I'm worried about Laurel. And I wondered if you might go look for her."

"What do you mean? I thought all you women went to the kitchen to help Reena."

Alexa shook her head. "That's all been taken care of. Laurel grabbed her coat and told me she needed to go to the barn. I tried to talk her out of it, but I couldn't get anywhere with her. And now she's been out there for ages! I'm worried about her. She's not acting like herself at all."

That damned calf, Russ thought. He thrust his coffee cup and dessert plate at Abe's granddaughter. "I'd appreciate it if you'd take care of these for me. I'll get my coat and go find her."

"Sure. And thanks, Russ."

Although March was almost here and spring would soon be coming, the nights here in the mountains were still frigid. As Russ crossed the ranch yard, his breath came out in big white puffs, and the snow-patched ground crunched beneath his boots.

Inside the big barn, he walked to the far end, where Laurel had housed the twin calf she was bottle feeding and, as expected, found her there. Apparently, it didn't matter that she was wearing a dress or high heels; she was kneeling over the animal and stroking its side.

"Laurel, what are you doing out here?"

Upon hearing his voice, her head jerked around, and

he could see by her look of surprise that she'd not heard him walk up, much less expected him to follow her to the barn.

"I'm making sure that Josie is okay. I gave her a bit more milk. And I was afraid she might get cold tonight so I turned the heat lamp on her."

So she'd already named the calf, he thought with misgivings. She knew better than that. He'd warned her not to name any animal that would eventually be leaving her care. It was easy enough to develop attachments even without names. Along with that, she'd already made a deep bed of warm straw for the animal, and nature had given it a heavy enough coat to handle the cold. But he wasn't going to start preaching to her tonight. Not when she looked so beautiful kneeling there in her dress and heels, with the heat lamp giving her hair a fiery-bronze sheen.

"I'm more worried about you getting cold," he said. "You're not exactly dressed for barn work."

"I'll be fine." She turned back to the calf and stroked its ears. "Josie already trusts me. She thinks I'm her mother now."

He stepped into the stall. "And you're a very good one, Laurel. But you needn't worry so about her. She's taken to the goat milk and is coming along nicely."

He stretched a hand down to her. "Come on, let's go back to the house. Alexa is worried about you."

Frowning, Laurel took his hand and allowed him to pull her to her feet. "I told Alexa exactly what I was going to do. She simply sent you out here to play matchmaker. Which was ridiculous, considering we're always working together."

His hand tight around hers, he pulled her close

against him. "Maybe she thinks we need some time together when we're not working."

Her lips trembled as her gaze made a hurried scan of his face. "I don't know what to think about you or us anymore, Russ. You haven't taken me to bed and—"

"I'm not going to, either," he said flatly.

"I should have guessed it wouldn't take you long to tire of me. Maybe if I was sexy like Alexa I could change your mind."

"Hellfire, Laurel, if you were any sexier it would kill me! And for your information, I'm aching to take you to bed. But without commitment from you—well, it would feel good. But it wouldn't feel right. Can you understand that?"

She placed her hands on his chest, and Russ couldn't decide whether she wanted to keep space between them or was inviting him closer.

"I understand that you want far more from me than I can give, Russ. That's why I've got to go away from here and find another job and forget I ever knew you!"

"I am not about to let you go anywhere!" he said with an angry growl.

Before he could stop himself, he wrapped his arms around her shoulders and bent her head back over his arm. But as soon as his lips swooped over hers, his anger vanished and he could feel nothing but desire and a desperate need to show her his love.

When her arms slipped around his neck and her mouth opened beneath his, triumph swept through him. Oh, yes, she wanted him. He could taste it on her lips, feel it in the way her body pressed into his. But that wasn't all he wanted. It wasn't nearly enough. And he couldn't settle for less.

Lifting his head, he stared down at her. "You don't

want to leave this job any more than you want to leave me," he said.

Tears pooled in her eyes, and then with a choked sob, she jerked out of his arms.

"Please thank the Cantrells for their hospitality. I'm going home!"

Russ didn't try to stop her. Instead he watched her race out of the barn as though she were being chased by a herd of demons.

"Lauralee, I've seen dead people that looked better than you," Maccoy said as he watched her pour a cup full of coffee.

As she stirred in a heavy dollop of cream, she cut her glance over to the older man. The afternoon had finally gotten quiet and he was now sitting at one of the desks, his chair tilted and his boots crossed on one corner.

"I missed my spa appointment this week," she said drolly.

"Okay, smarty, maybe a trip to the spa can put some color in your face. You're whiter than the sheet on my bunk."

"I'm fine, Maccoy, really. Just tired." In fact, she'd been exhausted ever since the dinner party a little more than a week ago. Stress, that's all it was, she'd been telling herself. Thoughts of Russ had been tearing her apart until she could hardly sleep, and eating was something she had to force herself to do.

The older man sighed. "Well, Russ thought we'd all get a little break from the hectic work pace when we moved out here to the ranch. But we've danged sure been busy. 'Course there's been some unusual situations that caused it, too. Like the bull gettin' through the fence to those heifers and causing all the early calves to drop. And then the sick cows. Russ is still workin' to figure out that problem."

Moving over to where he sat, she eased her hip against the corner of the desk. "Are you sorry we left the clinic?" she asked frankly.

"Hell no! Are you?"

Laurel didn't have to ponder on Maccoy's question. After all, how could she be sorry when she loved these mountains and livestock, her cozy little house in the woods and the camaraderie of the ranch hands. Even her pets loved their home in the woods, especially the dogs. As for her feelings for Russ, she couldn't blame this place for making her fall in love with the man, much less fall into his bed. Alexa had been right. She'd loved Russ for years. She'd just not wanted to admit it to him or herself.

"No. I'm not sorry."

"That's all you have to say about it?"

She shot him a puzzled frown. "What else am I supposed to say? I'm not sorry we're here. Period."

The older man let out a heavy sigh. "Damned, but you're a hard one to read. Maybe if you looked happy once in a while, I'd believe you, but—" He stopped, his eyes suddenly narrowed. "I've been expecting to see an engagement ring on your hand. What's happened?"

Totally stunned, Laurel straightened away from the desk. "An engagement ring?" She practically shouted the question. "Who— Why—"

He motioned with his hand for her to calm down and lower her voice. "Why are you gettin' all wild about a simple question? Russ told me he asked you to marry him. He told me you turned him down, but I figured you were smart enough to change your answer. Don't you think it's past time that you wised up?"

Her jaw tight, she tried to hold on to her temper. "Maccoy, I love you—but shut up! You don't know anything about what I should do."

"I might be old but that doesn't make me dumb. There's not one single reason you shouldn't marry the man!"

She arched a skeptical brow at him. "And you're an expert on the subject? A man who's never been married in his life?"

He jerked his boots off the desk and they hit the tiled floor with a loud plop. "Yeah, that's right! I was a fool and missed my chances. No wife. No kids. Nothing to be remembered by. Russ don't want that for himself and neither do you."

Her lips pressed to a grim line, Laurel walked over and tossed the remainder of her coffee in a trash basket. "I need to go give Josie her bottle," she muttered, then hurried out of the office before Maccoy could say more on the subject.

Damned old man, Laurel thought, as she entered the treatment room. *What did he know about it anyway?*

From what he'd said, Maccoy had allowed his chance to have a wife and family to slip away. Now he was alone and regretting it. Is that how she wanted it to be for her when, or if, she reached her seventies? A lonely old maid with no one to share the golden years of her life?

Trying not to dwell on those questions, she jerked a container of goat's milk from the refrigerator and poured a half gallon into a sterilized bottle. After she placed it in a bucket of warm water, she decided to walk down to the end of the barn and clean Josie's stall while she waited for the milk to heat.

At least the little girl calf had become a bright spot in Laurel's life. This past week she'd been eating voraciously and packing on weight. She was feeling so good, in fact, that she was bucking and racing around the small stall, especially when she saw Laurel coming with breakfast and dinner.

"Okay, Josie!" she sang out as she approached the calf pen. "Here I come."

Expecting to hear the rustle of straw, she was surprised when no sound greeted her. At this age, Josie did sleep a lot, but she was always awake at dinnertime.

"Josie?" She passed through the gate and into the stall, then suddenly stopped in shock. "Oh! Oh, no!"

The calf was lying stretched on its side, and from her long experience with animals, Laurel could quickly detect the little heifer wasn't asleep—it was in distress.

Cold fear washed over her as she raced over to the animal and collapsed to her knees. Josie was still breathing, but her respiration was rapid and there appeared to be some sort of white froth around her mouth.

Oh God, oh God, she prayed. *Don't let my little girl die!*

Her hands shaking violently, she jerked out her phone and punched Russ's number. He answered it after the second ring, and her voice was breaking with sobs as she tried to speak.

"Russ, please come quick! Josie—something is wrong. Hurry, please!"

"Laramie and I have just returned to the ranch yard. I'll be right in."

In less than a minute, he was striding into the stall with his medical bag in hand, and though she wanted to throw herself sobbing against his chest, she swallowed down her tears and forced her work experience to take control.

"When did this happen?" he asked quickly as he knelt over the animal.

"I just found her like this. I was getting her bottle ready and came down to clean her pen."

"Have you noticed any scouring today?" he asked as he quickly checked the heifer's eyes and nose and beneath her tail.

"No. She hasn't had scours at any time. The goat's milk has totally agreed with her."

He pulled out a stethoscope and listened to several spots on Josie's side. While he continued to examine the calf, Laurel checked the small water trough. "The water looks clean and fresh," she told him.

"Collect a sample of it," he instructed. "I want to test it and the goat's milk for bacteria. But first I want to get her started on an IV."

He rattled off the medications he needed, and Laurel hurried to the treatment room to collect them. By the time she returned with the bag, he'd already drawn several blood samples and affixed a needle to the animal. Now he quickly attached the tubing and adjusted the flow of fluids.

As Laurel hovered nearby, she wanted to throw several questions at him. Mainly, would the baby live? But she kept them bottled inside. Her job wasn't to distract the doctor with questions he might not be able to answer; it was to assist him and be an extension of his capable hands.

Biting down on her lip, she looked away and blinked at the hot moisture in her eyes. Getting attached to an animal was a no-no. It was one of the first things she'd learned when she'd started working at Russ's clinic. But Josie was different. She was a twin that had been separated from her sister and mother, just as Laurel had been separated from hers. Foolish or not, she'd seen herself in the little heifer and had instinctively become its mother. Now it looked as though she might lose Josie, too.

Russ straightened to his full height and looked at Laurel. "I'm going to the treatment room to have a look at the blood. Have you noticed the calf staggering or going around in a circle?"

"No. But a few hours have passed from the last time I looked in on her until now. Why? Do you think she might have the same thing as the sick cows from the mountain herd?"

"I see some similarities. Hopefully the blood will give me some clues. Right now I can't tell you straight out that she's going to live. I'll do everything I can. It's going to depend on how she responds to treatment."

Laurel swallowed hard as emotions formed a hot ball in her throat. "Is there— What can I do for her now?"

"Nothing. I want you to go home."

Her chin jutted forward. "No! I'm not leaving her."

"You're as pale as a sheet and about to drop." After picking up his bag, he walked over to where she stood. "Laurel, you don't have to tell me how you feel about Josie. But I want you to rest. I'll take care of your little girl. Trust me."

"I'll come back tonight and stay with her."

He shook his head. "You'll stay away from this barn until the morning," he ordered. "If anything changes I'll let you know."

As she swiped a hand over her face, she realized she was too drained and weary to argue. "Okay. I'll do what you say." She lifted her gaze to his. "And I'm sorry for getting emotional."

His features softened as he curved a hand tightly over her shoulder. "Oh, Laurel," he said gently, "you don't have to apologize to me for having a heart. Not this time."

He understood, she thought. *Really understood!* And suddenly her heart was swelling, filling with a love that was so deep and intense she was stunned by it.

"Thank you, Russ." She kissed him on the cheek and hurried out of the barn.

At home Laurel tried to make herself rest, but she ended up pacing restlessly through the house until bedtime. Then, once she'd gone to bed, she'd tossed from one side of the mattress to the other.

Her mind refused to shut down long enough to get one minute's sleep. Something had happened to her when she'd found Josie sick. Suddenly she'd been thrown back to her childhood and she was seeing Lainey sick and dying, her mother packing and walking out the door, and her father unable to give her any kind of emotional support.

And then Russ had walked into the stall, and just the sight of him had been like a steadying hand, a rock when everything else was falling to pieces. At that moment it had struck her that he was a man who would never crumble or leave. He would be there to hold her hand, to keep her standing through anything and everything. Why had it taken her so long to realize this? Why had she been trying to run away from the man instead of running to him?

Now she desperately wanted to be with Russ and little Josie. She wanted to tell them how much she loved them. Hopefully it wasn't too late with Russ. As for Josie, she could only pray that he could make her well again.

At midnight she checked her phone for messages.

There was one from Russ that simply read, Unchanged. After that, she tried to doze, but every few minutes she would jerk away and glance at her phone.

By five o'clock that morning, she could stand it no longer. She jerked on jeans, pulled a flannel shirt over a thermal top and tied her hair in a ponytail. Once she'd fed her pets, she hurried outside to her truck and headed down the mountain.

During the past week the weather had warmed considerably and melted all the snow. As a result the roads were muddy, and each time Laurel tried to speed up, the truck would slip and slide.

Finally the ranch yard came in view, and though it was still dark, she could see a thick curl of smoke coming from the bunkhouse chimney. Two cowboys were loading feed sacks onto a flatbed truck, while a row of saddled horses were already tethered and waiting at a hitching post.

As she passed the horses, she slackened her speed, then gunned the truck on to the treatment barn. Once she parked and leaped out of the truck, she didn't bother going to the office to see if anyone was there. Instead, she trotted to the end of the building where a door would lead her close to Josie's little pen.

Terrified at what she might find, she drew in a deep, bracing breath before she stepped inside the barn. But as she moved forward, a sense of peace came over her. No matter what happened with Josie, she thought, she could bear it, because Russ would be with her.

Squaring her shoulders, she walked from the shadowy alleyway and toward the glow of dim light pooling over the calf's pen. As she grew closer, she tried to peer over the board fence, but it was too tall for her to see anything. Or maybe nothing was inside, she thought.

Maybe Josie had died and Russ had already taken her somewhere.

Opening the gate, Laurel stepped inside the pen, then stopped short at the sight before her. Russ was sitting on the straw, his legs stretched out in front of him, his back resting against the board fence. Josie was lying against his outer thigh, her nose partially propped upon his knee.

Beneath the brim of Russ's hat, she could see his eyes were closed. As for Josie, she appeared to be breathing at a normal, restful rate.

Moving over to them, she lowered herself to the straw and gently touched Russ's shoulder. His eyes immediately flew open and focused on her face. As Laurel gazed back at him, the warmth of her love glowed in her eyes.

"Laurel. What are you doing here?" he asked, his voice gruff with sleep. "I told you to stay away until morning."

"You must have slept for a while, because it's nearly daylight," she told him.

"I remember Gus stopping by sometime in the night and then I must have fallen asleep."

Suddenly remembering the calf at his side, Russ quickly grabbed the stethoscope that was already resting around his neck and fastened it to his ears. Laurel watched anxiously as he carefully listened to Josie's heart and lungs and digestive sounds.

When he finally lifted his head and pulled the instrument from his ears, he looked at Laurel with faint amazement. "It's hard to believe, but she's much, much better."

Hope blossomed on Laurel's face. "Oh, Russ, does that mean she's going to survive?"

"She's made it through the worst of it and turned the corner. I can't see her taking a back step now."

Stemming the urge to squeal with joy, she looked at him through a haze of happy tears. "I love you, Russ Hollister."

The puzzled frown on his face was almost comical. "What did you say?"

"I said, I love you, Russ Hollister," she repeated.

Easing away from the calf, he grabbed her hands and quickly drew both of them to a standing position.

"Are you saying this because of Josie? Because you're grateful to me for saving her?"

She met his gaze with a confidence she'd never felt in her life. "This has nothing to do with Josie. Although I am very grateful that you're getting her well. I'm saying this because I've come to realize that hiding from the truth won't fix things or save me from being hurt. This thing with Josie has made me see that life is always going to be filled with disappointments, losses and trials." She lifted her hand to his face and wondered why it had taken so long to find the courage to open her heart and let him truly come in. "Before, I had always believed that if I was ever faced with another situation like Lainey's, I couldn't hold up to it. I believed I had used up all my emotional strength on her and would run away from the problem like my mother had."

Groaning, he pulled her into the tight, loving circle of his arms. "Laurel, you are a strong woman. You prove it every day. Working in this business, at my side, you've gone through plenty of heart-wrenching situations. You've always stood strong. You've never broken down or run away. I've always been proud of you, Laurel, and I love you. Very, very much."

"Russ. My love."

He was kissing her when she felt something nudging the side of her leg. Pulling her mouth from Russ's, she looked down, then yelped with surprise.

"Russ, look! It's Josie. She's standing! She's telling her mommy she wants her milk."

Laughing, he smacked a quick kiss on her lips, then released his hold on her. "Okay. I'll forgive her for the interruption this time. Go fix her bottle, and after she has her breakfast, we'll have ours. Then you and I have a lot of planning to do."

Happiness shining in her smile, she gave him one last kiss, then, leaving the stall, she called back over her shoulder. "Maybe we can talk Reena into making us some bacon and eggs. I want—"

Her words were suddenly cut short as her head begin to whirl and a rushing noise exploded in her ears. She thought she heard Russ calling her name right before she crumpled onto the straw in a dead faint.

When Laurel woke a few minutes later, she was on the couch in Russ's office. As her eyes focused, she realized he was bending over her, his face full of concern.

"What happened?" she asked groggily. "I remember getting dizzy and then my legs went all mushy."

"You fainted. And I'm taking you to the hospital to be checked out."

His announcement was enough to push her straight up to a sitting position. "No! Josie needs feeding and—"

"Maccoy just brought in a pail of fresh milk. He's going to take care of Josie's feeding," he assured her.

"Well, I'm fine now. You're a doctor. You can see for yourself that my vitals are back on track."

"Your vitals are clearly on the mend," he agreed. "But something caused you to faint. To keep you healthy, we need to know the reason."

She anchored her hands on his broad shoulders. "Russ, what if I have Lainey's blood disease?"

"Don't think in those terms, darling. Whatever it is, we'll deal with it together."

Days ago she might have panicked at the idea of being seriously ill. But not now. Not with Russ at her side. "I'm not worried," she told him. "Kissing you would cause any girl to faint."

Smiling, he scooped her up in his arms. "We'll put that theory to the test later."

More than two hours later, Russ sat in the Sierra General emergency room and thought what a cruel twist of fate it would be if something should take Laurel from him now. Now that she'd finally agreed that the two of them should be together.

But he couldn't allow himself to think in terms of losing. His mother had taught him that real love couldn't be measured with time. And though he'd felt desperately cheated when Nan Hollister had passed on, so early in his young life, he'd matured beyond that hurt. Instead, he'd grown to realize what a blessing she had been, how she'd guided and encouraged and inspired him to be the man he was today. She'd taught him that love was a precious gift, no matter if a person had it for one day or thousands.

"There he is. Over there—in the black hat."

At the sound of Laurel's voice, Russ turned his head to see the love of his life walking toward him with a young, dark-haired nurse strolling close at her side.

Jumping to his feet, he rushed over to the two women. "Laurel, my God, you've been back there forever!"

"That's the way with you damned doctors. You don't

care how long you keep a patient waiting. Especially when she's starving," Laurel teased.

"Are you sure you don't want me to push you out to the curb in a wheelchair, Miss Stanton? We don't want you to faint again before you have the chance to eat."

Laurel smiled at the pretty nurse. "Thank you. But Russ will let me lean on him."

The nurse smiled coyly. "I don't blame you. He's much nicer than a cold chair." She gave Laurel a quick hug and a short wave. "Take care of yourself. And congratulations."

Russ watched the nurse walk away, then turned a confused look on Laurel. "What did she mean by that? Was she congratulating you for not being sick?"

"Let's go over here and I'll explain." With a hesitant smile, Laurel led him across the wide room to a quiet alcove where no one else was seated. After they were both seated on a green couch, she went on, "I'm not what you'd actually call sick, Russ. Thank God my blood tests are fine. That's why it took so long—the doctor wanted to make sure everything looked right. He didn't have time to do in-depth testing, but he could tell from the initial results that I'm perfectly healthy."

"Really? Perfectly healthy women fall over in a dead faint?" he asked with skeptical sarcasm. "The man must be a quack!"

Laurel couldn't stop a laugh from bursting out of her. "Well, the quack just told me I'm pregnant. That's why I fainted. That, plus the fact that I've not eaten in twenty hours!"

Russ's eyes grew wide with disbelief. "Pregnant! Then you're not ill?"

Beaming now, Laurel shook her head. "Believe me, it was the last thing I was expecting the doctor to tell me.

Like I told you, I take the Pill, but he says if I go back and look I'll probably find I've missed one or took one out of turn. Or he said stress sometimes throws a woman's cycle so out of kilter, and a pill can't overcome the change. And God knows I've experienced some stress here lately."

A mixture of relief and concern continued to parade across his face. "But Laurel—you said you didn't want children. How do you feel about this news?"

She clutched his hands. "I said all of that out of fear, Russ. Before I realized how stupidly I was looking at things. Having your child is— It's the most wonderful thing I can imagine. I've never been so excited or happy in my life." The smile suddenly fell from her face. "But how do you feel, Russ? We're not yet married. And I assured you I was protected against pregnancy."

Suddenly he was laughing a deep, rich laugh that vibrated right through to her soul.

"The baby was meant to be. Just like you and I are meant to have a long, happy life together."

Epilogue

A month later, the family room in the big Chaparral ranch house was filled with a huge group of family and friends enjoying drinks and appetizers while they waited for dinner to be served. Tonight was a double celebration of sorts. Abe was having his eighty-fifth birthday, while Laurel and Russ had been married for three blissful weeks. And because they'd eloped and gotten married in a beautiful old mission up in Santa Fe, they'd missed out on having a wedding reception with their friends. Tonight's dual fiesta was meant to make up for that.

In the past month the ranch had finally seen winter giving way to spring, and the first tender blades of grass were beginning to grow on the river valley that stretched through the ranch's property. The mature cows were dropping their calves without problems, and the mares continued to add to the crop of babies that would eventually become a part of the Chaparral's working remuda.

As for Laurel, she'd chosen Quint's sister-in-law, Bridget, to handle her prenatal care and eventual delivery of the baby. So far the beautiful redhead had declared Laurel and baby to be in fine health. At first, Laurel had been half afraid Russ would try to make her quit work, but thankfully he'd seemed to understand how important her job was to her. Instead, he took extra caution to make sure she didn't do too much lifting or overtire herself. Laurel had never felt so loved or pampered in her life.

Pulling her thoughts back to the present, Laurel watched from her seat on the couch, as Quint carried his glass to the middle of the room.

"I think we should make a toast to Grandfather," Quint announced to the guests. "May he have many, many more nights like this one."

The white-haired man with his drooping mustache and wise, leathery face raised his glass and responded to his grandson's toast. "Thank you, Quint. And to Russ and Laurel for a long and happy marriage."

"Hear! Hear!" Frankie Cantrell seconded.

Laurel dutifully sipped her ginger ale, then turned to Russ, who was nestled comfortably at her side. "I've never seen Alexa and Quint's mother looking so beautiful and happy. Texas is definitely agreeing with the woman."

"Maybe she's found a man there," Russ said thoughtfully.

Laurel shot him a clever look. "A man? Does every woman have to have a man to make her happy?"

"I'm seeing a smile on your face," he smugly pointed out.

Laughing, she squeezed her husband's hand. "But not every woman is lucky enough to have a man like you."

Slipping his arm around her shoulder, he chuckled in a low, sexy way. "Hmm. Flattery. So what could you be wanting? To bring Josie home with us?"

Laurel grinned. As much as she'd loved her little cottage, as soon as she and Russ had married, they'd moved all of her things into his bigger house, including her cats. Leo was still outraged by the intrusion, but the arrogant tom was beginning to relent and make friends with the other felines.

"As much as I'd like to bring her home with us, she wants to play with the other calves."

"We'll turn her out tomorrow," he promised. "So she and her sister can get back together."

Laurel cast him a hopeful glance. "It will be okay for that to happen now?"

"The twins have grown past their very needy stage. They can eat grain and hay now, and the mother doesn't have to provide as much." He smiled at her. "See, they're going to get to be one big, happy family after all."

Sighing with contentment, she smiled at him, then swept her gaze around the room at all the people who were slowly and surely filling up her life in a very good and special way. This time Jonas had gotten to accompany Alexa to the Chaparral, and the couple appeared to be as much in love now as they had four years ago. Maura had just announced that she and Quint were going to have a third child and, incredibly, after all these years, Reena had received a warm letter from her daughter, Magena. "I guess we've proved my mother wrong," she said. "Happy endings do really come to pass."

The slight pressure from Russ's hand urged her gaze back around to his face.

"Speaking of your mother," he said, "I think you should call your father and brother and let them know about your marriage and the baby."

With a doubtful scowl, she said, "I'm not sure they want to hear happy news. They're all about doom and gloom."

He patted her hand. "If anyone can change their attitude, you can, my darling. And eventually our child will want to meet the only uncle and grandparent he or she will probably ever have. That is, unless your mother or my father miraculously reappear."

Laurel mulled that thought over for a moment. "You're right, Russ. My father and brother's dark look at life can't hurt me anymore—it can only hurt them. And maybe it's time they faced up to the way they treated me and Lainey. As for my mother and your father, I feel very sorry for them."

He arched a brow at her. "Why is that?"

"They gave up the best things in life they could ever have."

Bending his head next to hers, he nuzzled her ear and whispered, "You're going to make one hell of a good mother. And I'm a very lucky man."

"Well, still behaving like honeymooners, I see."

At the sound of Quint's teasing voice, both Laurel and Russ looked up to see the ranch owner taking a seat in a nearby armchair.

"Honeymoon?" Laurel asked jokingly. "What is that?"

The rancher chuckled. "Don't blame me. I've tried to send Russ away to Hawaii or somewhere nice and warm. But he's a workaholic and refuses to go."

"We'll go soon. Before the baby comes," Russ promised. "Right now there's still too much calving and foaling going on. And I don't want to go anywhere until we figure out who could be poisoning the cattle."

A perplexed frown creased Quint's face. "Who? I thought the question was what."

Russ said, "I was going to tell you later tonight. After supper. This evening I got a call from the university with the test results on Josie. The goat milk was tainted with a chemical substance. The same chemical substance that was found in the blood of the sick calves."

Floored by this news, Quint stared at him. "But couldn't that be from a fertilizer, or something inadvertent like a weed or poisonous vegetation?"

"It could. But it wouldn't explain Josie's milk being tainted. If the goat had eaten something poisonous and passed it on in her milk, she would have been deathly sick first."

Clearly horrified by this information, Quint shook his head, then darted a glance over his shoulder to where his wife, mother and sister were all gathered around Abe. "I can't imagine anyone hating us Cantrells that much."

"Maybe it's not about hating at all," Russ commented. "People do strange things for strange reasons."

Quint shoved out a long, heavy breath. "Well, we can only hope the twin calf will be the last incident we see of this. Right now I've got more immediate problems with Grandfather. His cook and old ranch hand, Jim, has broken his leg and is going to be out of commission for at least a couple of months. Grandfather refuses to leave Apache Wells and come to the Golden Spur to live with Maura and me and the boys. Now that Maura's expecting again, he doesn't want to put any extra work on her. He's insisting that Reena move out to Apache Wells and cook his meals. The damned man. He's just using Maura's pregnancy as an excuse to get his way, that's all."

Russ exchanged a knowing smile with Laurel. "Sometimes a man will do most anything to get what he wants."

This comment had Quint scooting to the edge of his seat and staring at Russ with disbelief. "Are you saying Grandfather has his eye on Reena? That's ridiculous! The man is eighty-five years old. I mean, sure, he's always liked women. But Reena is thirty years younger than him. And Abe's always said he's still in love with Grandmother's memory."

"Maybe he's put her ghost to rest," Laurel suggested, then turned an adoring look on her husband.

Loving Russ had finally given her the strength to put Lainey's ghost to rest, and though Laurel would never forget her beloved twin sister, Lainey's memory no longer haunted her.

Russ gave her a conspiring wink. "Don't worry about it, Quint. Could be Abe just wants to eat Reena's good cooking."

With a good-natured groan, Quint rose to his feet. "Either way, I think I'll go keep my eye on Granddad."

As the rancher walked away, Laurel turned to Russ. "I don't think he's too wild about the idea of Abe finding a new love."

"It's not about love—it's about change," Russ reasoned. "He wants his grandfather to stay just as he is."

A thoughtful smile curved Laurel's lips. "When you first told me you were moving here to the ranch, I thought the change would ruin everything. I was so very wrong."

His eyes sparkling with love, he squeezed her hand. "I felt a calling to this ranch and its family, Laurel. But most of all I felt a calling to be your husband."

"Well, you and your calling certainly changed me,"

Laurel said softly, "and all for the better. Sounds like Abe is in for a change, too."

Russ chuckled. "We'll soon see."

Leaning her head close to her husband's, Laurel sighed with happy contentment. "And we'll soon have another big change when our baby gets here. Think you're ready for it?"

"I couldn't be more ready, darling. You, me and our baby. The best is yet to come."

* * * * *

Don't miss the next story in the
MEN OF THE WEST *series, as*
Laramie meets his match!
Coming soon!

COMING NEXT MONTH from Harlequin®
Special Edition®
AVAILABLE SEPTEMBER 18, 2012

#2215 THE MAVERICK'S READY-MADE FAMILY
Montana Mavericks: Back in the Saddle
Brenda Harlen
Soon-to-be single mom Antonia Wright isn't looking for romance, single dad Clayton Traub only wants to make a new start with his infant son, and neither one is prepared for the attraction that sizzles between them....

#2216 A HOME FOR NOBODY'S PRINCESS
Royal Babies
Leanne Banks
What happens when a Texas nanny learns she is the biological daughter of a prince? Her rancher boss steps in to help protect her from the paparazzi, but who can protect her from her attraction to him?

#2217 CORNER-OFFICE COURTSHIP
The Camdens of Colorado
Victoria Pade
There's only one thing out of Cade Camden's reach—Nati Morrison, whose family was long ago wronged by his.

#2218 TEXAS MAGIC
Celebrations, Inc.
Nancy Robards Thompson
Caroline Coopersmith simply wanted to make it through the weekend of her bridezilla younger sister's wedding. She never intended on falling in love with best man Drew Montgomery.

#2219 DADDY IN THE MAKING
St. Valentine, Texas
Crystal Green
He'd lost most of his memories, and he was back in town to recover them. But when he met the woman who haunted his dreams, what he recovered was himself.

#2220 THE SOLDIER'S BABY BARGAIN
Home to Harbor Town
Beth Kery
Ryan fell for Faith without ever setting eyes on her. Their first night together exploded in unexpected passion. Now, he must prove not only that the baby she carries is his, but that they belong together.

You can find more information on upcoming Harlequin® titles, free excerpts and more at www.HarlequinInsideRomance.com.

HSECNM0912

REQUEST YOUR FREE BOOKS!
2 FREE NOVELS PLUS 2 FREE GIFTS!

♦ Harlequin®

SPECIAL EDITION
Life, Love & Family

YES! Please send me 2 FREE Harlequin® Special Edition novels and my 2 FREE gifts (gifts are worth about $10). After receiving them, if I don't wish to receive any more books, I can return the shipping statement marked "cancel." If I don't cancel, I will receive 6 brand-new novels every month and be billed just $4.49 per book in the U.S. or $5.24 per book in Canada. That's a saving of at least 14% off the cover price! It's quite a bargain! Shipping and handling is just 50¢ per book in the U.S. and 75¢ per book in Canada.* I understand that accepting the 2 free books and gifts places me under no obligation to buy anything. I can always return a shipment and cancel at any time. Even if I never buy another book, the two free books and gifts are mine to keep forever.

235/335 HDN FEGF

Name	(PLEASE PRINT)

Address	Apt. #

City	State/Prov.	Zip/Postal Code

Signature (if under 18, a parent or guardian must sign)

Mail to the **Reader Service:**
IN U.S.A.: P.O. Box 1867, Buffalo, NY 14240-1867
IN CANADA: P.O. Box 609, Fort Erie, Ontario L2A 5X3

Not valid for current subscribers to Harlequin Special Edition books.

Want to try two free books from another line?
Call 1-800-873-8635 or visit www.ReaderService.com.

* Terms and prices subject to change without notice. Prices do not include applicable taxes. Sales tax applicable in N.Y. Canadian residents will be charged applicable taxes. Offer not valid in Quebec. This offer is limited to one order per household. All orders subject to credit approval. Credit or debit balances in a customer's account(s) may be offset by any other outstanding balance owed by or to the customer. Please allow 4 to 6 weeks for delivery. Offer available while quantities last.

Your Privacy—The Reader Service is committed to protecting your privacy. Our Privacy Policy is available online at www.ReaderService.com or upon request from the Reader Service.

We make a portion of our mailing list available to reputable third parties that offer products we believe may interest you. If you prefer that we not exchange your name with third parties, or if you wish to clarify or modify your communication preferences, please visit us at www.ReaderService.com/consumerschoice or write to us at Reader Service Preference Service, P.O. Box 9062, Buffalo, NY 14269. Include your complete name and address.

HSE11B

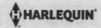

What happens when a Texas nanny learns she is the biological daughter of a prince? Her rancher boss steps in to help protect her from the paparazzi, but who can protect her from her attraction to him?

Read on for an excerpt of
A HOME FOR NOBODY'S PRINCESS
by USA TODAY *bestselling author Leanne Banks.*

Available October 2012

"This is out of control." Benjamin sighed. "Well, damn. I guess I'm gonna have to be your fiancé."

Coco's jaw dropped. "What?"

"It won't be real," he said quickly, as much for himself as for her. After the debacle of his relationship with Brooke, the idea of an engagement nearly gave him hives. "It's just for the sake of appearances until the insanity dies down. This way it won't look like you're all alone and ready to have someone take advantage of you. If someone approaches you, then they'll have to deal with me, too."

She frowned. "I'm stronger than I seem," she said.

"I know you're strong. After what you went through for your mom and helping Emma to settle down, I know you're strong. But it's gotta be damn tiring to feel like you've always got to be on guard."

Coco sighed and her shoulders slumped. "You're right about that." She met his gaze with a wince. "Are you sure you don't mind doing this?"

"It's just for a little while," he said. "You mentioned that a fiancé would fix things a few minutes ago. I had to run it through my brain. It seems like the right thing to do."

She gave a slow nod and bit her lip. "Hmm. But it would cut into your dating time."

Benjamin laughed. "That's not a big focus at the moment."

"It would be a huge relief for me," she admitted. "If you're sure you don't mind. And we'll break it off the second you feel inconvenienced."

"No problem," he said. "I'll spread the word. Should be all over the county by lunchtime. No one can know the truth. That's the only way this will work."

Coco took a deep breath and closed her eyes as if preparing to take a jump into deep water. "Okay" she said, and opened her eyes. "Let's do it."

Will Coco be able to carry out the charade?

Find out in Leanne Banks's new novel—
A HOME FOR NOBODY'S PRINCESS.

Available October 2012 from Harlequin® Special Edition®